INVERCLYDE LIBRARIES

WITHDRAWN

D0272902

Not What it Seems

Not What it Seems

Pamela Fudge

ROBERT HALE · LONDON

ISBN 978-0-7198-0960-6

Robert Hale Limited
Clerkenwell House
Clerkenwell Green
London EC1R 0HT

www.halebooks.com

2 4 6 8 10 9 7 5 3 1

Typeset in 11/17pt New Century Schoolbook
Printed by TJ International, UK

This book is dedicated to the dog owners I meet on my twice daily walks on the woodland and heath behind my house, making even walking in the rain a pleasure – and to all the pets who keep us fit and happy including Georgie, CJ, Stanley, little Ted, Jess, Titch, Harry, Digby, Colin, Benjie, Lacey, Charlie and Bella who became such friends of my own little Gizmo and have warmly welcomed Honey into their midst.

ACKNOWLEDGEMENTS

My thanks, as always, go to all at Robert Hale Ltd for the finished books that I am proud to call mine.

Grateful thanks go to Kay Whittington (paramedic) and to Dr Ken Galimore who provided lots of information and advice regarding the incident that occurs during the course of the story. I really wouldn't have had a clue and can't thank you enough.

To my wonderful family and friends I can only say that you make my world a better place and I love you.

One

We must have looked like any other couple, standing anxiously on the edge of the pavement outside our home in the small town of Brankstone, as we waved the youngest member of the family off to start a new life at university. Appearances can be deceptive, though, because our relationship quite definitely was not what it seemed.

Straining to catch one last glimpse of the bright-yellow Ford KA, I saw the matching teddy bear in the rear window tilt to one side, fall over and disappear from sight. The next minute the car had also disappeared around a bend in the road. For the longest time neither of us moved. This moment had been a long time coming and now that it was here I don't think that either of us quite believed it.

'That's it then, Evie,' Owen said, rubbing a hand across the bristles of his closely cropped fair hair and trying to sound matter of fact, 'the end of family life as we've known it.'

I thought I detected a slight wobble to his voice, though he was obviously making a valiant effort to keep his emotions in check. I didn't trust myself to speak at all, just stood there at the kerb and thought about the empty nest behind us – an empty nest with a For Sale sign standing outside.

The silence lengthened until I gave a little cough and found my voice. 'Time to put into place our plans for Life After Children,' I said firmly. 'They've been lying dormant for a very long time, but now it's time to get them out, dust them off, and put them into action. Isn't that right, Owen? And that,' I indicated the For Sale sign, 'is the first step.'

'Too right,' he said, injecting a hearty but transparently forced note into his voice.

It was only as we turned away from the kerb that I realized Owen still had his arm carelessly draped around my shoulders, and like that we walked towards the front door across the wide expanse of brick-paved driveway. It looked very empty with just my Beetle and Owen's four-by-four parked side by side in one corner.

'This is beginning to look like the supermarket car park after closing time,' he commented, as if he had read my mind.

'Room for a caravan and a horsebox.' I looked around and gave a businesslike nod. 'A good selling point the estate agent said.'

Owen's arm slid from my shoulders and we made our way slowly inside a house that seemed suddenly far too big and far too quiet. It was amazing the difference even the one remaining child had made, but it felt very odd without her already.

We knew there was a lot to discuss, even though we had discussed everything endlessly over the years. However, it soon became apparent that it was a discussion that was going to have to wait. The phone began to ring before I even had time to put the kettle on, as one after the other our other children phoned. In the end we decided it would be easier to go out.

Without even bothering to get changed, we switched off our mobile phones, snatched up a jacket each, and ignored the house phone, which was ringing again even as we closed the front door behind us. Grinning at each other ruefully, we climbed into the four-by-four, and I made a belated and futile effort to improve my appearance by dragging my fingers through the unruly tangle of my shoulder length fair hair as we sped off down the road.

'It's understandable that they're anxious, I suppose,' Owen said, once we were seated in our favourite Italian restaurant. 'Family life as we've all known it for so long is about to change forever.'

'Yes, but we've always been open and honest with them, so they understood from quite an early age that ours was just a convenient arrangement,' I pointed out, 'made for their benefit as well as ours. They're no longer children, but adults now, getting on with their lives. It's high time we got on with ours.'

'Fifteen years, though,' he marvelled. 'It's a long time.'

'I know,' I said, tucking into my favourite chicken and mushroom risotto with relish, 'who would have thought it?'

Owen had, predictably, chosen the same meal as me. He always did, wherever and whenever we ate out, and whatever was on the menu. I used to find it amusing and irritating in turn but, after all this time, I had stopped teasing him about it. I did still sometimes wonder, though, what he would do if I ordered something he really didn't like at all.

Scooping up a good forkful of the risotto, he paused with it halfway to his mouth. 'They've been good years, though, haven't they, Evie, on the whole?'

'Oh, yes,' I agreed immediately and, laughing, I added, 'and they said it wouldn't last.'

'Sandy and James?' Owen grinned, his face – tanned from working outdoors in all winds and weathers as a builder – lighting up. 'You're right, they did. They were absolutely horrified when we told them what we planned to do, said it wouldn't work in a million years, and blamed themselves because they were the ones who tried to pair us up.'

I smirked over the edge of my wine glass. 'You can just picture it, can't you? The perfect match, they must have thought. Get Evie round for a meal, she's divorced with kids.'

'And invite Owen. He's still on his own with his two, and he's been widowed for a while now.'

'I did like you straight away,' I told him, smiling, knowing I had told him the same thing many times before. 'I thought you were a really nice guy – kind and very nice looking.'

'Thank you. And I thought you were lovely.'

'But no spark,' we said in unison.

'Such a shame, especially as by the time we realized we weren't going anywhere as a couple, we'd been seeing each other quite a while and the children were all getting on so well,' I remembered. 'Luckily, we recognized the undoubted benefits of coming to an agreement that would help us both through what could have been some really difficult years.'

'It probably wouldn't work for everyone, but selling our

respective houses and moving in together was absolutely the right thing to do, wasn't it?' Owen asked, though he already knew the answer.

'Oh, absolutely,' I replied, without hesitation. 'We were already helping each other out but still couldn't have gone on for much longer, taking it in turns to drop the children off at yours or mine all the time. All of us being under the same roof made perfect sense, especially when they were so young.'

'Even in the bigger house it was a bit cramped to start with, though.'

'Like a hostel of some sort, at times, with bunk beds everywhere, but it was worth it in the end because the home we ended up with was the perfect family home – thanks to all your hard work.'

I never hesitated to give Owen the credit but, as ever, he insisted straight away that he couldn't have done it without me.

'Your homemaking skills were second to none, Evie,' he reminded me. 'Even when we ended up living in what wasn't much more than a builder's yard all those months, it was always as warm and welcoming as you could make it.'

I ordered tiramisu, my favourite dessert, as the empty plates were removed and, unsurprisingly, Owen followed suit. For a second I was tempted to change my choice at the last moment, but decided affectionately that it would only confuse him for no good reason and it was really quite endearing. After all they did say that imitation was the sincerest form of flattery, although whether that included food I really had no idea.

'Between us we've provided our children with a stable environment to grow up in.' I nodded, feeling a real sense of satisfaction. 'And we obviously did something right because no one could deny that they are a real credit to us.'

We tucked into the creamy puddings and thought about the family we had raised between us. The eldest two had already qualified respectively as a social worker and a physiotherapist, the third was currently studying to qualify also as a physiotherapist, the fourth to become a nurse, and the youngest was now enrolled on a midwifery course. Neither of us had any idea where the shared interest in health and social courses had come from but they each seemed happy with the choice they had made, so who were we to question it?

'Alice has often said that even the seasoned social workers have never heard of a family like ours,' Owen said, 'but I don't suppose we're unique, do you?'

I gave it some thought. 'Not unique, just a bit unusual,' and then I found myself staring hard at the door. 'Talking of Alice,' I said, hearing the surprise in my voice, 'I could swear that's her walking in right now but it can't be, can it?'

Owen twisted round in his chair, 'It is, you know, and isn't that Jake with her?'

My elder daughter flew across the restaurant and I found myself enveloped in a cloud of perfume and tousled blonde hair.

'We knew we'd find you here, didn't we, Jake?' She was laughing as she turned to Owen's son, and then her attention was straight back on us. 'I'll bet you thought you'd given us the slip, didn't you?' she said with a satisfied smirk.

'We weren't expecting you, were we?' I lifted my face to receive Jake's kiss.

'Alice was convinced you'd be feeling strange with Mai finally off to uni,' he explained, a smile lighting his handsome face. 'I did try to tell her you'd have become used to the family whittling away over the years, but she wouldn't have it.'

'Sit down,' I urged. 'Have you eaten? Well, join us for coffee then. Oh, it is lovely to see you both.'

Over the cappuccinos and skinny lattes, Jake said, 'End of an era, then? It felt really odd, seeing the For Sale board outside the house just now.'

'Are you *sure* you really want to give it up?' Alice suddenly sounded upset, I thought, despite the fact she hadn't lived at home for a number of years now.

'It's far too big, even for the two of us,' I pointed out.

'You could divide it into two flats.'

'That wasn't the plan,' I said gently.

'Plans are made to be changed, to be rearranged.' There was a touch of desperation in her tone. 'You get on so well, I really can't see why you insist on going your separate ways at your time of life.'

'Shush, Alice,' Jake pleaded, raking a hand through his dark hair and looking uncomfortable. 'It's none of our business.'

'Of course it is,' she argued fiercely, 'they're our parents. The only ones we remember, the only ones we've got. They should stay together for our sakes if not for their own.'

'People get divorced all the time,' Owen reminded her, 'and your mother and I aren't even married. We came together for *all* our sakes, for convenience, we aren't even in a relationship. You've always known we wouldn't be together forever, so this can hardly have come as a surprise to you.'

'But you're so *good* together,' she wailed, then did the only thing left to her and burst into noisy sobs.

I handed her a tissue from my handbag and tried not to notice the heads turning our way. 'Yes, we *are* good together because we are great friends – but friends is all we are, Alice, and all we ever will be. We've explained this to all of you over and over again. It's time now for us to start living our lives as the single people we actually are.'

'You'll get a good price for the house at least,' Jake said helpfully. 'Enough to buy a decent one each.'

'Don't,' begged Alice, sounding more like a child than a twenty-two year old professional adult.

'You have *your* own home in London,' he told her, 'and so do I.'

'*That*,' she said, 'is *quite* different,' but she dried her eyes and eventually – but somewhat reluctantly – joined in the chat about the various options open to Owen and me.

Neither of us wanted to move out of Brankstone. Owen had come to the area as a young bridegroom from his native Scotland and had built up a successful property maintenance business from its extremely humble start in a small shed at the end of his garden. He was well known locally and well respected. At forty-seven years old he didn't want or need to start again elsewhere.

I had grown up in the area, and life had seemed so simple when I'd fallen in love and married a local boy. However, my dreams of a happy ever after were dashed when – though we were already the parents of three beautiful children – my husband had decided that family life wasn't for him, after all and said he was leaving.

Kevin abandoned us so swiftly and easily that I was left in total shock and disbelief. As far as I was aware he had never once looked back. He did put the house in my name and continued to pay the mortgage, for which I was grateful, but that was the sum total of his commitment to the children and me. I had never set eyes on him from that day to this, had no idea where he was, and cared even less.

Thank goodness Owen had come into my life just when things were becoming pretty desperate. Needing to support my children, but with no family at hand to help out with childcare, there were times I hadn't known which way to turn. Owen's own need was as great as mine when, out of necessity, we had come together and made a life for our children together. I don't think either of us had any idea it was going to work so well.

Brankstone had always been mine and my children's home, it was all I really knew and now I had no desire to live anywhere else. It was fine that Owen felt the same and meant that when the children were on holiday we could share them between us in the smaller homes we planned to buy.

'A little bungalow would probably suit me,' I said, 'and I have looked at one or two online. Three bedrooms would suit, one for me, a spare for when any of you come to stay and one for an office.' I'd actually seen one that I thought would be perfect, but I didn't think Alice was ready to hear about that just yet.

'Finally going to write that novel with no one around to distract you?' Despite the fact that Jake wasn't even mine, he always had been the one to understand me best, and we smiled at each other.

'Something like that,' I agreed.

'I have an eye on an end of terrace,' Owen put in. 'Just a two up, two down, but it's on quite a big corner plot. I know I have the yard now and office premises but, who knows, I might want to wind down the business as I head towards retirement and become a one man band again, so it's as well to be prepared.'

'It sounds as if you have it all planned,' Alice said, quite bitterly I thought, and I felt a bit annoyed that she couldn't make an effort to see it from our point of view.

'Yes, well there's not a lot of time to waste "at our time of life",' I said, quoting her own earlier comment back at her, 'after all, we are both in our forties.'

'Well, when you're ready, we'll come and help you pack up, won't we, Alice?' Jake said cheerfully.

'*Will* we?' She gave him a straight look.

'You might all want to start going through things you left behind when you moved out,' I said, with a heavy emphasis on the last two words. 'I'm afraid that with both of us moving to smaller homes, it will be a case of "everything must go," as they say in the sales the shops are always having these days.'

'Yes,' Owen put in, 'there are a lot of books belonging to both of you, your collection of dolls, Alice, and Jake's Subbuteo.'

'Actually,' Jake laughed, placing the blame for the game

Owen mentioned squarely on my son's shoulders, 'the football stuff and any action man dolls you might find belong to Connor, and the wrestling DVDs and a boxed-up train set are mine, I think you'll find.'

Alice glared at all three of us, and I wanted to tell her it was difficult for us, too, but we were making the best of things and accepting that life just had to move on. Owen and I had tried to do our very best by our children over the years and I didn't think it was asking too much for them to return the favour now and make it easier for all of us.

Two

There was no sign of my daughter, Alice, on the day Owen and I moved to our respective new homes. I wasn't really expecting her to show up and I no longer even blamed her for the way she had reacted to the thought of us selling the family home and going our separate ways.

I had been quite prepared for the upheaval of moving, but even I hadn't expected the actual moment of leaving to be such a wrench. I found that I was absolutely dreading slamming the familiar front door behind me for the very last time.

I stood looking around the big empty sitting room, and recalled nursing five young children with measles on makeshift beds in there because it was the only room with a fireplace and the heating hadn't yet been installed.

Moving from there to stand in the kitchen, which had always seemed to be the hub of the house, I could still see them all sitting around the scrubbed old table in the early days, tucking into stew and dumplings with gusto, and I clearly remembered being absolutely thrilled to hear them laughing together. The memory still brought a smile to my lips – albeit a sad one.

'Not having second thoughts, are you, Evie?' I turned to find Owen standing in the doorway, smiling at me in the gentle way he had.

'It's a bit late for that, isn't it?' I queried with a little laugh, and shook my head. 'No, not me,' I said, adding, 'and not you, I would guess. We always knew that us all being together was a temporary arrangement – however long term – and not forever .'

'No regrets?' He came across the room and stood looking down at me with a touch of concern in his eyes.

'Oh, no.' I shook my head again, more emphatically. 'Putting our own lives on hold was a small price to pay to give our children stability. Stability we probably both needed every bit as much as they did at that time anyway.'

'Oh, God, yes,' Owen said with feeling. 'With no family around to help out when Susan died, it was a complete nightmare those first few months. Reliable childminders were non-existent. I don't know what I'd have done if you hadn't come along when you did.'

'Ditto,' I said with feeling.

'Here, give me one last hug.' He held out his arms and I went into them gladly, enjoying the security that being held like that always gave me.

'I hope it's *not* the last one,' I said laughing, and tried not to feel daunted by the thought of living alone after so many years as part of a family.

'It's not even goodbye,' Owen said, his light tone matching my own. 'We're hardly moving to opposite ends of the country.'

'No,' I agreed, fighting the urge to keep my arms around him even after he had let me go. 'Practically round the corner from each other, really.'

'This is it, then,' he said, when we found ourselves standing outside the familiar front door that, as of that moment, no longer belonged to us, 'I'd better go and drop the keys off ready for the new owners.'

The house had sold quickly. So quickly, in fact, that it had given us no time for second thoughts – even if we might have had any. I hoped the new family would be happy: they had seemed nice when they came to view and thrilled to find a home they said was perfect for them. I hoped it was, because it had been perfect for us.

'This is it.'

We walked side by side to our cars, exchanged a final quick hug, and in no time we were driving off in opposite directions. Concentrating on the unfamiliar route, it took me a minute or two to realize that my face was wet with tears. I hadn't gone much further before I had to pull over because I was crying so hard.

I'd heard all about the empty nest syndrome that caused some women so much grief and was determined it wasn't going to happen to me. I'd loved raising my extended family, but the children were well-balanced adults now, and making their own way in the world. I couldn't think what on earth was wrong with me. I should have been excited, happy, at the thought of a future that at last belonged just to me.

I was still young, barely forty-five, with my whole life in front of me. I'd been working towards this moment since the day Kevin and I had married, though I'd been happy to put my dreams on hold while we raised the family I had firmly believed we both wanted.

OK, so it hadn't quite worked out the way I had expected. I had ended up bringing up not one but two families, and with a man who had been little more than a stranger when we had first hatched our plan, but had quickly become my best friend in the world. Now it was time for Owen and me to go our separate ways – just as we had always known and accepted that, one day, we would.

I dried my tears and drove on, refusing to dwell on the fact that I had expected to spend my middle age – and old age, come to that – with Kevin and not on my own. After all, I didn't have to remind myself that Owen had visualized a very different future, too.

Life happens, I reminded myself severely, and you have to work with the hand that you've been dealt. In the end, given the circumstances, things couldn't have worked out better.

My spirits lifted the minute I drove through the open gates of my new home. Parking space for just two cars at a push, the driveway made of tarmac rather than brick paving, but here pretty shrubs grew against the fences of my very own boundary.

The key slid easily into the lock and turned. Silence enveloped me as I stepped inside and stood for a moment, looking around me, enjoying those first moments of real ownership and marvelling at how neat and tidy everything was already. A place for everything and everything in its place, as the saying went, and I would soon get used to not finding shoes scattered along the hallway or coats on the banister.

'What do you think?'

I almost jumped out of my skin and whirled round to find my son standing behind me watching my reaction. 'Connor, don't do that to me.' I placed a trembling hand to my heart and laughed shakily. 'I thought everyone had gone.'

'Everyone but me, Mum.' He pulled a hand from behind his back and held out a bunch of flowers. 'Only from the Tesco Express down the road, but I know you like yellow flowers.'

'That is sweet of you, love,' I said, reaching out to take them. 'Time for a cup of tea, or do you need to get off?'

'We—ell.'

'You go. You've got plans for this evening, haven't you?' I remembered, 'and you have that drive in front of you yet. Where's your car? It's not in the drive.'

'No, I parked it up the road because of the removal van. Not much room in a cul-de-sac, is there? Will you be…?'

'I'll be fine,' I told him firmly, then sobbed into the bunch of brightly coloured chrysanthemums as I watched my tall, fair-haired boy walk away and wondered what the hell was wrong with me. I never cried, and today I seemed to have done little else.

I put the flowers in water, boiled the kettle and made tea, then left it to go cold as I moved from room to room and tried to familiarize myself with my new home. It was exactly what I had visualized, two bedrooms at the front of the property, with a loft extension providing a third – though in this case the room would be my office, den, study. Call it what you will. It was going to be perfect for what I had in mind.

Unlike the house I'd left – which had needed so much to

be done to it when we moved in – now that the furniture had been moved in this bungalow was ready to live in. I viewed it with a critical eye, though. Owen and I had shared everything scrupulously and let the children take whatever they wanted, so it was looking a bit sparse in places.

The plain cream walls cried out for pictures, some pretty cushions should be scattered around, a few framed photos and perhaps a few tasteful ornaments, too, would make it feel more like home. Being more used to curtains, I wasn't sure what I felt about the vertical blinds, but knew I would probably grow used to them and shouldn't rush into making expensive changes.

What I did like very much was the open-plan kitchen, dining and sitting room at the back of the bungalow with French doors that opened onto the small rear garden. I went back in there, sipped the lukewarm tea and grimaced before pouring it away down the sink and flicking the switch to boil the kettle again.

I had wandered outside, and was reminding myself sternly that it was the wrong time of year to be thinking about garden furniture, despite the unseasonably warm weather and a desire to do everything at once, when I heard my mobile ring.

'Mai,' I said, delighted to hear from my youngest daughter. 'How are you? How is the course going?'

'It's fantastic, Mum.' She sounded bright and happy. 'The midwifery tutors are lovely and we've already formed into quite close groups according to our clinical placement areas. We'll be out on community from next week.'

'So soon? Are you looking forward to it?'

'Oh, yes, and … but that's enough about me. What about you? Are you in?'

'I am,' I said proudly, looking around again with a smile, 'and pretty well straight already. Connor helped – and Ella, of course.' Ella was Owen's daughter, and she and Mai had bonded very quickly as children, with only the one year between their ages.

'Oh, good. She did promise she would try. No sign of Alice, then?'

'Well, she's really upset, you know.' I excused my eldest daughter.

'That's Alice, always thinking of herself,' Mai said shortly, and then hurried on, sounding even crosser. 'She seriously wants to be thinking about things from your point of view for a change, and to try to remember the huge sacrifice you and Owen made for us all those years ago.

'I still can't believe everything's happened so fast, though.' She sounded impressed. 'You two didn't hang about, did you, once I was off your hands – and that's not a criticism,' she hastened to add before I could say a word. 'Connor and I were saying how much you deserve this new start after all you've done for us.'

'Thank you.'

'It was always difficult for my friends to believe you and Owen weren't what you would call a "proper" couple, because you always got on so well together – better than most of their parents if they were to be believed. I had to keep saying, "It's not what it seems, you know".'

'I know,' I said ruefully, 'I've spend the last fifteen years saying the same thing.' I shrugged, though I knew Mai couldn't see me. 'People will always believe what they want to anyway, in my experience. *We* all knew the truth.'

'Did you never, in all that time, ever think it might become the real thing?' Mai asked the question they had probably all wondered at one time or another, but I could tell from her tone that she hesitated to pry.

'No.' The word was firm. 'We were and are just good friends – nothing more and nothing less and, after all these years, we both know that isn't going to change.'

I thought I heard her say, 'Pity,' very quietly, but I could have been mistaken.

The thought, once it had been put in my mind, wouldn't seem to go away. I ate cheese on toast while flicking through TV channels, made a grocery list and then another list of items I wanted to buy for the bungalow, but – probably because of Mai's comments – Owen's face kept popping up in front of me.

It was actually a very nice face, as I already knew, and I had no idea *why* I didn't fancy him, but I never had and that was nothing but the truth. Yet he had all the attributes I'd have ever looked for in a man. Tall, fair-haired, fit, always tanned from working outside a lot of the time, better looking than the majority of the men that I knew, he was also a really lovely guy, with a delicious sense of humour, and he was pretty placid, too. Well, he'd have had to be to share a house all those years with five children of a similar age and me.

But, no, there was nothing. My heart had never once skipped a beat at the sight of him, and whether he was wrapped only in a towel after his shower, or he was dressed up in his best suit, it made no difference. He was just Owen.

Living in such close proximity, he'd seen me at my best and worst, too. He'd often brought me a cup of tea in bed in the mornings – and boy, was I going to miss that, I realized with a sudden pang of regret – nursed me through more than one bad dose of flu and even helped me to highlight my hair a time or two. He'd zip me into a dress and then stand back and tell me I looked nice, but there was no real gleam in his blue eyes that might hint of anything more than fondness. I'm not sure what I would have done if there had been, because it wouldn't have been reciprocated.

We'd each had our share of dates over the years, but in the end they seemed to be more trouble than they were worth, especially when it came to explaining our relationship and living arrangements. I never met one guy who didn't look askance at me, as if I would actually lie about something so important.

In the end, our social life centred round our growing children and the friends who knew and accepted us just as we were. Looking back, I supposed we actually *were* a couple, of sorts, but without all the complications that reared their ugly heads whenever sex was involved.

The more I thought about it, the more I realized how very lucky we had been. All our energies over the years had been able to go into rearing the children and it had been a truly wonderful time – especially because we both so appreciated the security our arrangement had given us at a vulnerable time in our lives when we had so badly needed it.

I shook myself mentally and reminded myself that all good things came to an end. The children were a credit to us, each following the career path they had chosen and as well balanced as any youngsters I had ever met. Our work was done and it really was time for a change.

Three

I slept fitfully in my new bedroom, feeling unexpectedly lonely. Even after Kevin had left I'd had the children for company, so it felt really strange knowing that I was living completely alone for probably the first time in my life.

I'd not actually shared a bed with a man since Kevin, but from the time Owen and I merged our two families and shared a house I'd felt totally secure in the knowledge that he was only just across the landing. Many was the night that a fretful child had woken us both and, while one comforted, soothed and resettled, the other had been downstairs making tea. I had always slept more soundly just knowing he was there – now that comfortable sense of security was missing.

I didn't feel nervous exactly – though I had carefully double-checked all the doors and windows before I went to bed – just a bit odd. I reminded myself that I had known it was going to be very different because going in a relatively short time from a large house, literally heaving with people, to a small bungalow with only me in it was a huge step. I was sure I would soon get used to the very noticeable differences, but was still glad when morning came.

I ate cheese on toast again for breakfast because all there was in the house was bread, milk, cheese, and tea bags. Not even any butter. What on earth had I been thinking? I realized I had been a bit too quick in encouraging Owen to help himself to the groceries from home.

No, I corrected myself swiftly; *this* is your home now.

I wasn't about to starve. I had plenty of time to go shopping. It was half-term so I had no teaching commitments. The sun shone on a beautiful October day, and barefoot I wandered outside onto the decking with a slice of cheese on toast in one hand and a mug of tea in the other.

I could actually *feel* my spirits lifting as I pictured the table and chairs I would buy in the spring and be able to enjoy in the summer. The hedges surrounding the garden gave absolute privacy, so I would be able to sit out here, undisturbed, writing notes for my book on sunny days or relaxing with a glass of chilled wine and a good book on warm evenings.

I jumped then as I noticed a little black thing – obviously an animal of some sort – in the corner of the garden. I fought my first instinct, which was to run indoors, because it obviously wasn't a rat, and I stared at it in fascination. What on earth was it? The creature was the size of a small cat, but didn't look much like one. It had a pretty face, quite fox-like, and was very fluffy.

'Hello,' I said, 'who are you?'

It barked then, so apparently it was some kind of dog, though I'd never seen one quite like it before.

'Gizzie, Gizzie.' The voice filtering through the hedge was a man's and sounded quite elderly.

'Hello,' I said again in the general direction of the voice. 'If you're looking for your dog, I think I've found him.'

'Oh, I'm sorry, he's found his way through the gap again. He's looking for Winnie. She used to feed him titbits.'

'Shall I bring him round?' I asked.

'Oooh, no,' he said hastily, 'don't touch him. Gizmo doesn't know you and might well nip if you try and pick him up. I'll come and get him.'

I went to unbolt the side gate and waited for my neighbour to reach me. My first impression was of a gentleman in his seventies, very upright and quite slight of build. A bright smile lit his lined face as soon as he saw me, and as he got closer I detected a real twinkle in the brightest pair of blue eyes. I couldn't help smiling back, knowing instinctively we were going to get on.

'Arthur,' he told me, seizing my hand in a firm grip.

'Evelyn,' I returned, adding, 'Evie to my friends. Excuse my undressed state.' I indicated the long dressing gown and bare feet. 'I haven't been up very long.'

'I won't keep you,' he promised. 'Just catch my dog and go.'

It quickly became apparent that Gizmo had no intention of being caught as he led his elderly owner a merry dance, prancing away the minute Arthur got anywhere close.

'Little varmint.'

I suspected Arthur was using stronger language under his breath, and hid a smile.

'Why don't I make a fresh pot of tea and give you a chance to catch your breath before you have another go at catching your dog?' I offered, feeling all this ducking and diving wasn't good for a man of his advanced years. 'Gizmo obviously thinks you're playing with him and he might just come to you on his own if you leave him alone.'

Arthur sank down on a low garden wall, so I took that as a yes and went inside to put the kettle on. While it was boiling I went back to say, 'I can offer you cheese on toast to go with the tea, but nothing else because bread and cheese are all I have.'

From the pleased look on his face you'd have thought I'd offered a banquet. Arthur accepted that and my offer to step inside with alacrity. Sitting at the dining table, he looked around.

'My,' he sounded impressed, 'I can't believe the change in the place.'

'How do you mean – with different furniture?'

I put the tray on the table and took the seat opposite the first visitor to my new home. Out of the corner of my eye I saw a little black face peering in through the door, and drew Arthur's attention to it.

'Yes, I expect he'll come right in by and by if we ignore him.' He looked around again before explaining, 'Winnie's son went to town on this place when his mum went into the nursing home, knocked down a couple of walls, built that extension at the end there.' He indicated the sitting room that continued on from the dining room. 'Made another room up in the loft and generally spruced the place up. If you want to see how it used to look you can take a look at mine some time.'

Gizmo had come right inside by this time and was looking

at me quizzically. I held out my hand and he sniffed my fingers cautiously, then the tail, which I hadn't noticed curled along the dog's back, began to wag and a tiny pink tongue came out to lick my fingers.

'Give him a wee bit of that cheese, Evie, and you'll have a friend for life,' Arthur advised.

I did as I was bid and asked, 'What kind of dog is he? I don't think I've ever seen one quite like it before.'

'A Pomeranian,' the old man said, adding knowledgeably, 'they were bred down in size from the German Spitz for Queen Victoria to have as lapdogs apparently.' He screwed up his nose. 'Not a man's dog, really, but he belonged to my late wife and she thought the world of him. He's company and walking him gets me out and about.'

'How long have you been on your own?'

'Two years and I still miss her every day. You're on your own, are you?'

'Yes, but from choice.' I realized that that sounded a bit harsh and felt obliged to explain. I hadn't meant to say more, but before I knew it the details of my complicated previous living arrangements came tumbling out of my mouth in a rush. Bless Arthur, he didn't even blink, but took everything I said at face value.

'Sounds as if you both took the common sense approach and solved all of your immediate problems in one fell swoop,' he said, 'and did a lot better than those who fall in and out of love and swap partners so often that the kiddies don't know where they are.'

I beamed at him, because he was about the only person I'd ever met who'd seen only the benefits of our arrangement and didn't just jump in to criticize. I found myself offering: 'More cheese on toast?'

'Don't mind if I do,' he said, pushing his plate forward. Gizmo had settled next to his feet under the table by this time and was sound asleep with his nose resting on his little paws.

'Have you lived here long?'

'Most of our married life – sixty years we celebrated just before Rose passed on.'

'*Sixty*?' I was incredulous. 'Do you mind me asking how old you are, Arthur?'

'I'll be eighty-eight next birthday.'

'Good grief,' I exclaimed, 'I'd have taken at *least* ten years off – especially the way you were chasing Gizmo around that garden.'

'Bless you.' He looked pleased. 'Our son is fifty-nine. He lives in Australia with his family.'

'That's where my family live, too: my mum, dad and my sister and her family. The three of them emigrated years ago and I stayed behind because I was newly married. We've grown apart and I don't have a lot to do with them, I'm afraid. In fact, I can't recall the last time I spoke to them.'

'When he first went out there we had to depend on letters and the occasional phone call,' Arthur explained. 'Then I kept in touch through email, but it's easier for me since the couple the other side of you helped me to get onto Skype recently.'

'A silver-surfer,' I exclaimed, impressed, 'and an advanced one at that.'

'I had to go off and buy a computer and then join a class to learn how to use it.' Arthur tucked into the fresh slice of cheese on toast that I had put in front of him and chewed thoughtfully for a moment. 'But, as I told Rose, we must move with the times. She had no interest at all, though she always read Ronnie's emails once I'd printed them up. It broke her heart when he emigrated and I know she found it difficult to accept that he had his own life to live. It was not seeing the grandchildren that upset her the most.'

'I'm sure,' I sympathized, wondering how I would feel if even one of my children moved away. 'Well, you're way in front of some of my students,' I told him, explaining: 'I teach creative writing to adult learners and some of them are still under the impression that publishers will happily read handwritten manuscripts.'

'You're a writer?'

'Mmm. In the early days it was mainly textbooks and articles on office procedure, which did quite well. I was an office manager for a small company, you see, before I married, but I always had a flair for writing. I could work from home and it fitted in well when the children were small and gave me an income, but I was always interested in writing fiction. Eventually I tried my hand at that as well and have had some success with the short stories I've written for magazines over the years. My plan, now that I have only me to worry about, is to write a novel.' There, I had said it out loud and Arthur didn't even laugh at my lofty ambition. I found I was becoming fonder of him by the minute.

'Well ...' he began, but at that moment the doorbell went and roused Gizmo, who barked furiously.

'He's a good guard dog.' I smiled. 'Especially as it's not even his house. Excuse me a minute.'

Conscious that my hair hadn't even been brushed, I smoothed it ineffectually on my way to open the front door and tightened the belt of my dressing gown.

'Owen.' I opened the door wide, really pleased to see him.

'I just called to see if you wanted to come out for breakfast.' He looked at my undressed state and added, 'I can wait while you get ready.'

'Oh, that would have been lovely,' I began, 'but I've got a guest and we've already eaten breakfast.'

'Oh.' Owen sounded surprised, shocked even.

I was about to add that he was welcome to come in and join us, but he had already turned on his heel and was making his way back down the path.

'You don't have to rush off, do you?' I called after him.

'A lot on,' he said abruptly.

The next minute he had climbed into his four-by-four and roared off leaving me to close the door slowly and wonder what on earth his problem was.

'That was my ...' as always I found myself hesitating over Owen's correct title because there wasn't really one that fitted our unique circumstances, 'friend.' Before I elaborated: 'It was Owen, the guy I used to share a house with.'

'He's not coming in?' Arthur asked, looking as if he might have quite enjoyed someone else to talk to.

'No, he said he had a lot on.'

'Yes, and I expect you have a lot on, too,' Arthur said, getting to his feet a little stiffly and gathering up Gizmo. 'I did enjoy the cheese on toast and the chat, but you needn't be afraid I shall be making a nuisance of myself and be forever popping round.'

'Nothing was further from my mind,' I assured him. 'It's been lovely meeting you both and I shall know where to come when I need to borrow a cup of sugar.'

'I don't take it myself,' he said with a twinkle, 'but I'll be sure and keep some in.'

By the time I'd had my shower and headed off out with my shopping list, I had convinced myself that Owen had spoken nothing but the truth. He did have a lot on and was probably relieved that his offer of breakfast had not been accepted. It was just like him to make time in a very busy day for such a kind gesture, aware, as he would surely have been, that I had very little food in the house.

I returned hours later, having spent the best part of the whole day in the huge Sainsbury's just outside town, eating my lunch there before I began a mammoth shop the likes of which I hadn't undertaken since my days of catering for five children and two adults. You needed most of the same grocery items for one person as for a family, I discovered, just smaller amounts.

Besides buying enough to stock up my store cupboard, fridge and freezer, I'd even managed to buy photo frames, cushions and a couple of ornaments that might help to make my pristine home look a bit more lived-in. I found the sheer variety of what could be bought in a supermarket these days amazing, and was only too happy to be able to take advantage. One-stop shopping certainly had a lot to recommend it, I decided, as I made my way home.

I was still in the process of transferring bags from the car to the house when Owen suddenly appeared by the side of me.

'Oh, *am* I glad to see you,' I said with feeling, and handed him a couple of loaded carrier bags. 'You're just in time to give me a hand.'

'What happened to the *guest*?' he said, obediently following me inside and looking around.

'Oh, he went home hours ago,' I said blithely. 'Just put the bags down over there. I'll start unpacking once they're all inside.' Then I plodded outside again and repeated the process a couple more times with Owen following me backwards and forwards silently.

'You're welcome to chat while I put the stuff away. I can still listen,' I encouraged. I had worked my way through several bags, finding homes for the contents, before I realized he still hadn't said a single word. 'Cat got your tongue?' I asked in the end.

'Something like that,' he replied in a clipped tone that was very unlike his usual lazy drawl.

I stopped what I was doing and faced him. 'What's up?'

'Well ...' he said, and then stopped.

'Come on, out with it,' I said chirpily. 'Something bothering you?'

'Well ...' he said again, and paused. This time I didn't prompt him, just waited for him to go on. 'I know it's none of my business....'

'But...?'

'But you certainly didn't waste any time, did you, Evie?'

I just looked at him, and when he didn't elaborate I said,

'I'm sorry, but I don't have a single clue what you're talking about.'

'If it was someone you've been seeing recently, why haven't you said? We've always been honest with each other.'

I gave his words some thought, and then said, 'No, sorry, but I still don't have a single clue what you're talking about.'

'Oh, for God's sake stop playing the innocent with me. It isn't clever and there's absolutely no need to be so secretive. It's me, Owen, and I know you too well.'

I just stared at him, shook my head and shrugged my shoulders.

'This morning,' he spoke slowly, as if I was really stupid or something, 'you opened the door in your dressing gown with your hair all over the place, and informed me, as cool as you like, that you'd just had breakfast with "a guest".'

The penny finally dropped with a deafening clang and I wanted to laugh. Instead I began to explain, 'Oh, that was—'

'Spare me the details, Evie,' he snapped nastily. 'You can say it's none of my business, but—'

I kind of lost it a bit then. Suddenly this wasn't funny and I didn't like his tone. I didn't like it at all.

'You're right,' I snapped back, 'I *can* say it's none of your business, because it damn well isn't. I don't have to explain myself – or any "guests" I might entertain – to you and I'm not going to. Thank you for your help with the bags. You can go now.'

With that I marched past him to the front door and stood there pointedly holding it open. Without another word he left and I slammed the door behind his back. Then I stood there staring at it.

'*What*,' I said out loud, 'was *that* all about?'

I put the rest of the shopping away, going over and over what had been said and managed to come up with only one conclusion.

'Was it possible he was *jealous* – of *Arthur*?' I asked myself and then roared with laughter at such an absurd notion.

Four

I didn't actually laugh for long before the anger came back and wiped the smile from my face.

Where Owen might have gained the impression that I had to keep him informed of any changes to my life and the people in it, I wasn't sure. We had always known that at some point we would be moving on and living separate lives. We had discussed and agreed numerous times – as a family – that that point would have been reached as soon as all of the children were old enough to be doing the same.

Since it was something we had all been totally aware of throughout the years we had shared living under one roof, and was also something neither of us – or the children – had ever questioned before, it made Owen's current behaviour and Alice's, too, all the more inexplicable.

There had never been any question in any of our minds that Owen and I would remain what we had always been – and that was the best of friends. However, his peculiar conduct couldn't be excused on the grounds of friendship as far as I was concerned. I couldn't understand it, or excuse it at all. I would have stated categorically that he didn't have a possessive bone in his body and I couldn't believe that that could have changed overnight just because we were now living apart.

Thankfully a telephone call with some unexpected news distracted me or I might have wasted hours of my time pondering on Owen's strange behaviour and what lay behind it.

I'd snatched up the ringing phone fully expecting to hear a sheepish Owen on the end of the line ready to offer a grovelling apology. However, the deep voice, though pleasant, was definitely unfamiliar.

First checking my name, he then continued, 'Well, Mrs Clark, this is Bill from Brankstone Carpentry and Joinery. I'm just contacting you because my boss has asked me to let you know we've just finished the last job ahead of time and he's said that, if it's all right with you, we can be round at yours first thing in the morning to make a start on your home office.'

'Really?' I was shocked. If I was being honest I was far more used to tradespeople arriving either days later than agreed or not at all. 'You can start tomorrow?'

'Yes, tomorrow – if that's OK with you.'

'But that's brilliant, a whole week ahead of schedule. I'll see you tomorrow, then. Is there anything I need to get in?'

'Tea and coffee would be great.' I could hear the smile in the man's voice. 'Biscuits would be a bonus.'

The minute I got off the phone I raced up the stairs and stood in the middle of the loft conversion, trying to picture it with the brand new office fittings in place. I had been quite happy to make do with furniture from the family house for my new home; there had been more than enough and to spare for Owen and me to each furnish our much smaller homes. However, this room was to be my one luxury, and it had been meticulously planned and designed to my own specifications the minute I knew the bungalow was going to be mine.

Obviously originally planned as an extra bedroom, this room even had an en suite, so it was going to be just about perfect. I felt a smile creeping gradually across my face and growing until it stretched into one huge beam of pure delight.

The following morning I was awake far too early on what promised to be a grey day, but I already knew it was going to take more than a bit of cloud or a spot of rain to dampen my enthusiasm. I literally bounced out of bed, showered, dressed and was already looking forward to the day ahead. Having plenty of time I'd enjoyed a leisurely breakfast, and then started getting ready for the workmen. I'd boiled the kettle for tea, the coffee was perking and I was reaching for the mugs when I noticed Gizmo patrolling the garden. I wondered if Arthur had realized yet that he was missing. Knowing how worried he would be if he couldn't find the little dog, I hurried outside.

'Arthur, are you there?' I called, unable to see through the dense and neatly clipped Leylandii hedge.

'He's over there, is he?' the old man surmised. 'That's a relief, I was afraid he might have got out the side gate.'

'I'll close the back door and open the front one. Just come round when you're ready. There's no hurry, he seems quite happy.'

I put the door on the latch for him and went back to pour

sugar into a bowl and put biscuits on a plate. I was once more reaching for the mugs when I heard the door close.

'Come on through, Arthur,' I called, and when there was no reply I turned to find it was Owen standing behind me.

'Had his breakfast and coming back for his elevenses now, is he?' he said sourly, eyeing the plate of biscuits and the tray currently holding just two mugs.

Before I could think of a cutting reply, the doorbell went and, pushing past him, I went to answer it. Fully expecting to find Arthur on the step, instead I found myself face to face with a very fit guy, probably about my own age, wearing a T-shirt and jeans and carrying a toolbag.

'You're early.' I beamed.

'We aim to please,' he said with a grin. 'This way, is it?' he asked, and was already making his way straight up the stairs before I could suggest a tea or coffee.

If they were always this eager to get started, I reasoned, it was small wonder they completed jobs before time. I was still smiling when I went back into the kitchen and found Owen still standing in the same place with a huge scowl firmly in place.

'He's keen,' Owen said, as if that was a crime.

'Isn't he?' I agreed, refusing to be riled.

'Like I said before, you haven't wasted much time, and is that a dog out there?' He indicated the garden with a nod of his head.

'It is.' I didn't add that it wasn't mine.

'Not much of a man if that's his dog,' he said disparagingly.

'And that would be any of your business because...?' I folded my arms.

'...Because I care about you, obviously.'

I almost said he had a funny way of showing it, but I wasn't rising to anything he could say this morning. I had decided that on my way back from opening the door to Bill.

'I care about you, too.'

'Thank you.' He said it as if he didn't believe me.

'But,' I continued, as if he hadn't spoken, 'you don't find me on your doorstep making disparaging remarks about your visitors.'

'That's because I don't have any – yet.'

'Well, perhaps you should change that and then you wouldn't be quite so interested in mine,' I returned swiftly.

'Oh,' he harrumphed, 'there's no talking to you.' With that he turned on his heel and left, slamming the front door – *my* front door, I thought with annoyance – behind him.

The doorbell rang immediately and I whipped it open ready to demand what the bloody hell he wanted this time, only to find another very nice-looking guy on my step. This one I recognized, since he was the one who had planned and priced my new office.

'Something eating him?' He nodded a head towards Owen's vehicle as it roared away, once again, from my property. 'He nearly took my van door off.'

'And nearly this one off its hinges,' I said ruefully. 'Must have got out of the wrong side of the bed – not mine,' I added hastily in case he got the wrong idea, 'I live alone. It's Stuart, isn't it?'

He nodded. 'Is Bill here yet, Mrs Clark?'

'Upstairs – and I prefer Evie.'

'Excellent. We can start bringing everything in – and I prefer Evie, too,' he added with a smile.

'Tea or coffee before you both get started?' I offered.

'You obviously know how to get the best out of your workmen. I can already smell the coffee brewing. We'll make a couple of trips while you get it ready and then take a ten minute break.'

Arthur followed them through the front door as they hefted pieces of wood up the stairs and couldn't wait to ask me what was happening.

'My study/office/den – whatever the in word is for such a space – is being constructed ahead of time,' I told him, allowing my pleasure to show. 'Isn't that great?'

'You won't know yourself,' he told me, sharing in my excitement. 'Rose made Ron's old bedroom into a sewing room – she was a dab hand with a needle or sewing machine,' he added by way of explanation, 'but it's empty now, and you saying what you're having done upstairs has started me thinking I could do something with it and maybe make a little office of my own.'

He accepted my invitation to join us for coffee and was soon chatting away about his own very recently hatched plans for an office to Bill and Stuart, with Gizmo sitting under the table happily accepting the tiny pieces of biscuit surreptitiously being slipped to him by the two carpenters. They seemed as taken with the dog as he was with them.

'Want us to come round and give you a free estimate?' Stuart offered, reaching down to pat the little dog's head. 'We do pensioner's rates.'

'I think that would be too grand for me,' Arthur said, while thanking him for the kind thought, 'and show up the rest of the place. 'No, a nice old desk and filing cabinet would be good enough – and perhaps a bookcase, because I do have a fair few books. Too many, really; Rose was always on at me about cluttering the place up with them. She'd be pleased to see them tidy.'

He left soon after to be there for his grocery home delivery. I was impressed at how he seemed to manage so much of his life online.

'Nice old boy,' said Stuart thoughtfully.

'Are you thinking what I'm thinking?' Bill queried.

'That office we refurbished? Yes, I was. We never did get round to getting rid of the furniture we removed and I think it might be just what he'd be looking for.'

'Oh, that is kind. I'd be happy to pay for it,' I said.

'We wouldn't want paying. It's really just cluttering the place up. Happy to bring it round, but are we sure he would really want it?'

'It would be lovely to surprise him,' I mused, 'but I would imagine Arthur is very proud. Tell you what, leave it with me and I'll talk to him some more.'

With that they clattered back up the stairs and soon banging and sawing could be heard to a radio accompaniment, along with a bit of whistling and tuneless singing now and again.

It reminded me of those far off days when Owen was working as a self-employed builder during the day, and evenings and weekends on making the house we'd purchased between us into a family home big enough to accommodate two adults (unattached) and five children with ages ranging from three to eight years. I'll never know how he did it, but the result, after months of knocking down walls and adding an extension, was a beautiful house with six bedrooms on the first floor and big family-sized rooms downstairs.

Only our two youngest daughters, Mai and Ella, had to share a room but at three and four years old respectively they had no problem with that and continued to share even when the older ones eventually started moving out. They were still so close and so similar in their fair colouring that they were often mistaken for twins.

It was just a shame the two of them hadn't managed to gain places at the same university, but being a year apart and on different courses was bound to send them in different directions and perhaps that was a good thing – a good thing for each of us to find our own way in life and that included Owen and me.

Circumstances and necessity had put us all together – and I still shuddered to think how different and how difficult life would have been had I been obliged to struggle on alone – but it had been an elaborate arrangement which, though it worked beautifully for all of us, was never meant to be forever. Owen no longer had to feel responsible for me and so I would tell him next time he came poking his nose into my business.

I could feel my temper beginning to rise again, so I was almost relieved when Gizmo popped through the hedge and made his way confidently to my back door. He was quite happy for me to pick him up now, so I tucked him under my arm and made my way next door to return him to Arthur. It would, I decided, give me the ideal opportunity to mention the offer of a desk and see how it was received.

'Little devil,' was Arthur's greeting when he opened the door. 'I'm going to have to do something about that gap or he'll never give you a moment's peace. Bring him in and have a cup of tea with me for a change.'

It was interesting seeing how my own bungalow must have looked originally, with all the rooms separate and therefore much smaller, though this one did lack the clutter of many older people's homes – except the piles of books he had mentioned – and it merely looked cosy.

'He's no trouble,' I assured Arthur, adding: 'but when I go back to work next week I shall have to lock the side gate, so you won't be able to come round and get him back. I'm not sure how secure my garden is either, and I wonder whether he could get out onto the street. We wouldn't want that to happen, would we?

'Perhaps the guys next door can find a bit of spare wood to block the gap,' I suggested, and then continued, as if I'd just thought of it, 'they were saying just now that they had a desk and filing cabinet going begging at their yard. They brought it away after they fitted a home office, but it's just in the way. I wonder if it might be the kind of thing you were thinking of.'

'They haven't just said that because of what I mentioned earlier, have they, Evie?' he looked suspicious.

I laughed, 'Don't be daft, Arthur. They couldn't have just conjured up what you needed out of thin air. They haven't even left my house. Honestly, it sounded to me as if you would be doing them a favour – it would be a shame if what sounds like very serviceable furniture went to the tip.'

'Recycling centre,' Arthur corrected me automatically.

'Come round at about one o'clock and share a sandwich lunch and they can tell you about it themselves.'

'All right, I will,' he agreed, after fighting a very transparent battle with his pride. 'I'd be cutting off my nose to spite my face not to even consider it, wouldn't I?'

'Absolutely,' I agreed.

By the time he arrived, the guys had found the gap in the hedge and blocked it with a sturdy piece of wood. In a way I was sorry because I was already getting quite fond of the little black scrap of dog and his owner. I had to remind myself quite severely that soon I would be working and writing and would have to be more frugal with my time.

It didn't take Stuart long to convince Arthur that he would be doing them a good turn by taking the old office furniture off their hands.

'It might not be what you had in mind at all,' he told the older man honestly. 'It's obviously good quality, but old fashioned and bulky. Everyone wants lightweight and modern these days. Why don't you come round and have a look before you make a decision? Just be honest and tell us straight if it isn't what you want. I promise we won't be at all offended.'

'I'm a bit old-fashioned myself,' Arthur said with a touch of humour, 'and there's nothing in my house lightweight or modern, so it should fit right in. I will accept your generous offer and be grateful for it. The room has stood empty since Rose died and her sister carried off the dressmaking gear. Well, it was no use to me was it? Rose would have been pleased to see her things set to good use and she would be pleased to see the room set to good use again, too.'

'Nice old boy, isn't he?' said Bill, after Arthur left. 'Reminds me a lot of my wife's granddad. He's a bit of a character, too.'

'He's very welcome to the furniture, but what, exactly, does a man of that age want with an office?' Stuart didn't try to hide his curiosity.

'He's one of your silver-surfers and very computer literate,' I told them, as proudly as if he was my own father – and in fact I already felt closer to him than I had to my own father for many years. 'He regularly Skypes his son's family in Australia and, although I'm years younger, I've never Skyped in my life.'

'Nor me,' said Bill.

Stuart shrugged. 'I suppose you have to have a family there to Skype in the first place. I don't, do you?'

Bill shook his head.

I was silent for a long moment, and then I confessed, 'I do, but it would take more than Skype to make me want to talk to them.' Then, for some obscure reason, I burst into tears.

Five

I couldn't think what had come over me, getting all upset over a family I'd had no contact with in a very long time, and I jumped up and rushed about clearing the remains of lunch away to hide my confusion. Bill, obviously embarrassed by such a display of emotion, couldn't make himself scarce soon enough and quickly disappeared upstairs.

'Are you OK, Evie?' Stuart hovered, obviously uncomfortable, and looking as if he didn't know whether to bolt after his friend or stay and make some sort of attempt to comfort me. To his credit, he stayed.

'Oh, gosh, yes, I'm absolutely fine,' I insisted. 'I don't know what in the world came over me because I certainly don't miss them,' I added dismissively and with a conviction I was suddenly far from feeling. 'I haven't even thought about them in years.'

'Then perhaps you should,' he suggested before quietly leaving the room.

'It'll be all the upheaval, Evie,' Arthur said, nodding, when I went round the following morning to admire the office furniture that had been delivered by the boys first thing.

Dusty and a bit scratched it might have been, but I could tell that Arthur was thrilled to bits. I looked up from where I had taken over the polishing of what appeared to be a solid mahogany desk, using the real old-fashioned polish Arthur favoured and which the desk so obviously deserved, and stared at him.

'Moving house?' I asked. Despite myself and my muddled thoughts, I found I couldn't help enjoying the sight of Arthur sitting up very straight and turning himself slowly in a huge office chair so grand that it looked as if it might once have belonged in the Prime Minister's office at number ten Downing Street.

'That and the end of family life as you've known it for years. It's been quite an upheaval for you, Evie.' He stood up and went to slide open the top drawer of a full-sized filing cabinet, and nodded his satisfaction. 'This will be great,' he said, pushing the drawer in and pulling it out again a couple of times, 'for keeping all my paperwork in one place.'

'Lucky you, they've even left the hanging files in place so all you need is some labelled folders to keep things in order. I expect I'll have to buy everything new.' The duster I was wielding stilled on the bookcase that was presently bene-fiting from my attention, and I invited, 'Perhaps you'd like to come to Staples with me some time and have a look around – or you can look online and have everything delivered. You have your furniture – and very nice it's starting to look, too – but you'll want items like desk tidies. That's the thing you keep your pens in, and there are all kinds of other useful bits and pieces that you'll never know how you managed without.'

'I'm not going to know myself, am I?' Arthur's blue eyes

sparkled. 'It's given me a new lease of life having you next door, I can tell you, and you haven't been there for more than five minutes. You needn't worry that I'll be plaguing you all the time though, because I know you're going to be busy with your writing.'

'It looks as if you're going to be busy yourself.' I indicated his own little office space all ready and waiting, and asked suddenly, 'but who will you get to move your computer and set up the broadband connection again, Arthur? Because it's no good looking at me. I'll be looking for someone to set me up once my study is completed.'

'I'll have to throw myself on Giles Baxter's mercy,' he said with a slight grimace, adding, 'he's the neighbour on your other side and lives there with his wife, Ruth. They're a couple of what they used to call yuppies a few years ago. Both something important in the city, or so I'm led to believe. Always in a hurry, and rarely at home, but he'll do it for me with an air of martyrdom so that I'll be left in no doubt of how precious his time is. He won't charge, but I always give him a bottle of good whisky and thank him effusively. I have to say I am always very grateful for his help but it's not nice to be made to feel like a nuisance.'

In the end there was no need for us to throw ourselves on Giles's mercy; a huge relief because I didn't like the sound of him and hadn't been looking forward to asking such a big favour of someone I'd never met. It seemed the setting up of my computer would be done by an associate of Stuart, the cost being built in to the original price. He assured me that the same person would be only too happy to sort Arthur out at the same time for a bottle of good whisky.

He told me all this when I returned home from Arthur's, to be provided with the information that I'd had a visitor in my absence – obviously Owen – who had appeared none too pleased to have the door opened by one man, only to be advised that I had gone to visit another.

'Ex, is he?' Stuart asked sympathetically, adding, 'I've had one or two, myself, with stalker-like tendencies.'

'Not an ex, and hardly a stalker, just a good friend, so I'm not sure exactly what his problem is at the moment, but I'm sure he'll tell me eventually.'

'Perhaps he wants to be more than a friend, Evie,' he suggested, looking at me over the rim of his coffee cup.

'I doubt that. We've known each other for fifteen years, so if he wanted anything to develop I'm sure it would have become apparent before this,' I said firmly, and then changed the subject as Bill joined us.

With term starting in a few days I had other things to think about than what Owen thought he was playing at, and I certainly wasn't going to phone and ask him. With no access to the files on my computer – though I was sure that if I'd been more IT savvy there must have been a way of logging in somewhere else – I resorted to pulling out the arch files holding my previous year's lesson plans and schemes of work and made any necessary changes in pen. Luckily I kept plenty of copies of any course handouts so I didn't have to do more than be sure I had a pile of the appropriate ones ready.

The classes were quite established now, the faces familiar, though there could possibly be one or two new ones to join us. I felt the usual flutter of nerves as I ensured my briefcase held everything that it should and then excitement at the thought of the news my students might bring. Even with only half a term behind them, it wasn't too soon to have had a letter or article accepted for publication if they'd only had the confidence to make a submission.

Working with adult learners suited me admirably, and encouraging other would-be writers kept my own enthusiasm levels high. Being part-time and working only term-time also gave me ample opportunity to turn my attention to my own writing and my small successes bolstered my income as well as my confidence.

The thought of attempting a novel was daunting, and a previous attempt had resulted in only three pretty poor chapters before I'd run out of steam, but I had come to the conclusion that nothing ventured was nothing gained. I would never know what I could achieve if I didn't keep trying. I shouldn't be giving that same advice to my students if I wasn't prepared to take it myself.

The weekend passed without anything much of note happening and I found the house extremely quiet without the cheerful and industrious presence of my two joiners. I had steadfastly refused their constant offers to view the progress they were making upstairs and didn't attempt so much as peep around the door in their absence. Instead I made myself busy in the spare room downstairs, checking the contents of the boxes labelled 'office' and ensuring that those relating to computer hardware were arranged close to the door, all set for the guys to carry up ready for installation.

I was beginning to get quite excited at the thought of a

brand new space that was all my own. A laptop had never appealed to me, so it was going to be amazing to see my desktop PC actually set up on a permanent desk and to have a place for everything else after years of working at a table in a corner of the big kitchen.

I didn't have to remind myself that the makeshift arrangement had been my own choice once the children started leaving home, because I had steadfastly refused Owen's regular offers to turn one of the vacant bedrooms into a study. It had never seemed worth the effort when it would be such a temporary measure, so I always said that I could manage.

He was such a lovely man and nothing had ever been too much trouble for me and the children. It made me a little sad to think of him and his recent strange behaviour, because in no time at all he appeared to have turned into someone I didn't even recognize. If I'd been asked I would have stated quite confidently that even though we would be living separately, we would go on much as before. I had always visualized us popping in and out of each other's houses regularly – always sure of a warm welcome.

Well, I mused, I couldn't say he hadn't popped by, but he'd been so rude and belligerent each time that the thought of going anywhere near to his house was the furthest thing from my mind. I was reluctant even to pick up the phone – and after years of frequent daily contact between us that didn't feel right at all – yet every time my hand hesitated over the phone a vision of the last time I had seen him soon made me snatch it away.

Bored with my own company by the evening but not feeling inclined to cook, I popped to the fish and chip shop I had seen on the main road, stopping at Arthur's on the way to invite him round to share the repast with me. He didn't need inviting twice and followed me up the path when I arrived home with an excited Gizmo at his heels.

The plates had been warming in the oven and the bread was lavishly buttered. The contents of the paper-wrapped parcels were swiftly deposited onto the plates and we each drenched the generous portions with salt, vinegar and tomato ketchup and talked with our mouths full, not wanting the food to get cold.

'Mmm,' I mumbled, 'I know some would say it's probably bad for you, but I adore crispy batter and this is the best I've tasted in a long while.'

'Never did me any harm or Rose either, 'cos she lived into her eighties, you know, and we used to treat ourselves most Fridays.' He looked sad for a moment, and added, 'It never tastes quite the same when you eat it on your own so I'm really enjoying this.'

We both looked up then as the doorbell rang.

'Probably the Avon lady or someone collecting for charity,' Arthur guessed.

I don't know why, but I was taken completely by surprise to find Owen on the step, wearing a smile, his best suit and carrying an impressive bunch of flowers.

'Owen,' I said, staring at him as if we'd never met before. In actual fact, I didn't have to remind myself that this smiling Owen had been conspicuous by his absence of late.

'I'm really sorry,' he said humbly, thrusting the flowers towards me. 'I don't know what's got into me lately. I hope you'll let me make it up to you by allowing me take you out to dinner tonight. You're probably as fed up as I am by now with cooking for yourself.'

'Erm,' I hesitated, but knew I had to go on and reject his offer, 'apology accepted, but I've actually already eaten – am eating, in fact – but you're welcome to come and join us.'

'Us?' he repeated, his tone changing to the one I had come to dread, and as he spoke, Gizmo, who had been surprisingly quiet, burst into the hall and began to bark furiously round Owen's feet.

A sneer that was becoming rather too familiar of late appeared on Owen's face, and though he didn't actually kick the little dog, he pushed him away with the side of one polished shoe.

'Oh, I get it.' He looked at me with such intense dislike that it quite took my breath away and I took a step back and snatched up the dog.

'What's that supposed to mean?' I demanded, feeling my temper beginning to rise. 'What do you get?'

'That I'm already surplus to requirements. I don't know why I'm even surprised, because the house seems to be full of men every time I come here. You'll be getting quite a reputation, Evie.' With that, he threw the bouquet at my feet and turning on his heels made to stalk away.

For a moment, I wondered how many times that made in the short time I had lived here, and then I knew I wasn't going to let it happen yet again. This time I was going to put him right.

I think he was as shocked as I was when I went after him and, grabbing hold of his arm, wrenched him round to face me.

NOT WHAT IT SEEMS

'Not so fast,' I said, sounding every bit as furious as I felt. Standing behind him, and with my hand in the flat of his back I pushed him back towards the house and almost forced him through the front door.

'Don't,' I ordered, 'say one bloody word. Just take the door on the left there and go up the stairs behind it.'

Total surprise must have made him do as I bid and he climbed the stairs in silence with me close behind him, still carrying Gizmo. In silence we surveyed the half-finished office.

'Workmen,' I told him. 'Two of them, and thank you for spoiling the surprise for me, because I had intended waiting until my very first office was completely finished before I came up here.'

'Sorry,' he mumbled, but he was obviously determined to have the last word. 'A *workman*, is it, downstairs sharing your supper?'

By this time I couldn't even speak because I was so angry, but pushed him back towards the stairs and followed him down them. When he would have turned to the front door, I caught his jacket sleeve, spun him around and then, with a good shove to his back, sent him towards the back of the house. He was brought up short by the sight of Arthur sitting at my dining table still enjoying his fish and chips. The sight of mine going cold made me even more furious.

'Let me introduce you to Arthur. We're not exactly an item. Arthur is my lovely next-door neighbour and Gizmo is his late wife's dog.' I smiled, and I knew it wasn't a nice smile, 'You – of all people, Owen – should know everything is not always what it seems. I would ask you to join us, but I wasn't expecting you and we were enjoying our fish and chips far too much to share. Weren't we, Arthur?'

Arthur looked from Owen to me and then to the hefty portions of food still uneaten, but he wisely remained silent, just nodding a greeting towards Owen.

'Don't let us keep you,' I snarled, and taking the hint, Owen muttered, 'I'm sorry to have interrupted your meal,' and turned to go.

I followed him to the door, which had been standing ajar all this time, waited until he was through it and then picked up the flowers and flung them with all the force I could muster after him.

'Take your peace offering with you,' I advised, 'and don't come back until you can accept that what I do and who I see has absolutely nothing to do with you.'

I slammed the door so hard that it rattled. Then I set Gizmo on his feet and watched as he hurled himself against the door, barking furiously.

'Exactly,' I fumed. 'I couldn't have put it better myself.' I went back to join Arthur and a pile of stone-cold fish and chips.

Six

Some of the pleasure I had been finding in my new home and the new life I had planned was being spoiled for me by Owen's out of character behaviour, and I didn't think I could find it in me to forgive him.

Arthur pleaded with me not to be too hard on him, but I didn't understand why he would choose to stand up for him and told him so. Owen's conduct had been disgraceful since the day I'd moved in. I didn't hesitate to tell him so on each of the several occasions he phoned after that most recent disastrous visit, attempting feeble apologies. I simply put the receiver down after treating him to a few choice words – and then felt inexplicably bad about it.

The only thing that did put a smile on my face was returning from work one day to find my smart new office completed and everything up and running – ahead of schedule, of course. Even that was tainted by the fact that I had as good as been forced to view it half-finished just to prove to Owen that I wasn't entertaining a houseful of men – and I would still like to know what business it was of his even if I had been. It was perfectly acceptable for him to be concerned, but not for him to behave as if he was an outraged parent, and I the wayward teenage daughter.

The spare bedroom, cleared of the boxes of stuff intended for the office, eventually looked as immaculate as the rest of the house and the children – both Owen's and mine – began to come to stay for an odd night when they could get time away from their courses, with the notable exception of Alice. I comforted myself that it was already into November and she was bound to relent by Christmas, though she was very cool when I phoned her early one evening.

'I know you would have liked Owen and me to stay together, Alice,' I acknowledged, 'but we can't fall in love with each other to order, you know. If it was going to happen there's been ample opportunity over the last fifteen years. Surely you wouldn't expect us to carry on and maintain the status quo just for you children?'

'But it wouldn't just be for us, would it?' Alice said, in what I was sure she thought was an extremely reasonable tone. 'You surely can't like living alone, either of you.'

'Actually, I'm loving it,' I said, and then wished I hadn't when she said waspishly,

'Well, you obviously don't miss Owen or any of us either. That's really nice to know and there's obviously nothing more to be said,' before slamming the phone down.

I stood holding the receiver and felt like crying my eyes out. I'd obviously failed my elder daughter in some way, but I didn't quite know how. She was a grown woman, had been the very first child to leave, and hadn't lived at home for several years. I would have found the behaviour she was exhibiting more understandable in Mai, who was younger, had only very recently left home, and yet was far more accepting of the changed family circumstances.

I was actually relieved when the doorbell rang, but hoped fervently that it wasn't Owen looking for another confrontation or, indeed, my acceptance of yet another apology.

I was so pleased to find Stuart on the step that I was probably extra effusive in my greeting. Throwing the door wide and I ushered him in, offering: 'Coffee, tea, beer or you can join me in a glass of wine?'

'Unusual to get such a welcome when I arrive with my invoice,' he said, obviously taken aback. 'I take it you're pleased with your study and everything is working as it should.'

'Oh, yes, it's wonderful. I won't know myself – when I get the chance to make full use of it. At the moment the thought that Christmas is fast approaching is becoming something of a distraction and it's as much as I can do to find time to jot a few ideas down. I was actually expecting your bill to pop through the door long before this.'

Stuart accepted a beer; refusing a glass he drank from the bottle and looked very relaxed, leaning back against the kitchen worktop. He was tall, taller than I remembered, as good-looking as I recalled in a rugged kind of way, casually dressed on this occasion in jeans, T-shirt and a black leather jacket. I could feel him watching me as I poured myself a generous glass of chilled wine and felt suddenly self-conscious, which was plainly ridiculous given that it wasn't long ago that he'd been in and out of my house on a daily basis and seen me at my best and my worst.

'Classes going ok?' he asked, taking another sip of beer.

'Great,' I nodded, 'I already have a few small successes to add to my scrapbook. It's brilliant when that happens during the first term.' I went to one of the cupboards and reached for the cheque I had already written. I held it out to Stuart. 'I think that's what we agreed, but you must tell me if there were any unexpected expenses incurred.'

He stuffed it into the pocket of his jeans without looking at it.

'Don't you…' I began.

'I trust you,' he said abruptly.

'Do you want to take a look at your workmanship now that all my stuff is in place?' I offered, for want of something better to say or do. I managed to laugh. 'I've made a real effort to find a place for everything and put everything in its place and have even sorted my books into categories and alphabetical order.'

'Sounds good and I would like to see it. I don't often get to see the end results of our labour.'

I led the way and was very conscious that he was right behind me on the stairs. I really wished I wasn't wearing ancient boot-cut jeans and a washed out T-shirt that had seen better days. Had I known he was coming I'd have made a bit more effort, because I was very aware that as a middle-aged mother of three my figure, though still slim, was hardly perfect and I'd have chosen something a bit more flattering. I wasn't sure why I was bothered but, somehow, I was. Well, I had my pride.

The loft conversion was a big room, but the fitted furniture made it seem smaller and so did having Stuart prowling around, looking at the pictures and pin-boards on the walls and running his fingers along the books on the shelves.

He turned suddenly, and we came face to face, except that he was so tall I barely reached his shoulder and found myself looking up into eyes I hadn't realized until that moment were brown.

'It all looks great, Evie,' he said simply. 'The beech wood was a good choice.' Then suddenly, out of nowhere, he added, 'I would really like to take you out, and I would really like to kiss you.'

I took a step back, really quite shocked, because I hadn't seen this coming – not at all.

'Now I've offended you.'

'No, no, of course not,' I denied with a nervous laugh. 'Surprised me, flattered me, but no, I'm not at all offended. I would have thought I was a bit old for you.'

'I'm thirty-nine and you can't be more than – what – forty?'

'Forty-five.'

'I like older women,' he insisted and, reaching out, he took my hand and drew me inexorably towards him.

The feeling of his lips on mine was quite delicious. There was no other word for it. The stubble on his chin I had expected to be bristly and rough but, in fact, was amazingly silky against my skin, and his mouth coaxed mine to open under his with very little effort on his part. I was so out of practice that I felt like a gauche teenager, but he was the best teacher and I melted into his arms. For the first time in a very long time I gave myself up to pure enjoyment, reaching up to bury my hands in the thickness of his curly hair wanting the moment to go on and on.

'Mmm,' he murmured, drawing back eventually to look down at me. The look in his eyes made me go weak at the knees so that I was glad he was still holding me. 'I just knew you would be a great kisser. I've been driving myself mad thinking about it for ages.'

I just felt stunned and was glad to leave him to do the talking.

'But we're rushing ahead and you haven't agreed to let me take you out yet.'

'Yes, please, I'd like that,' I said honestly, and we both laughed a bit breathlessly.

'The ex, he won't mind?'

I went to say again that Owen wasn't my ex and anyway it was absolutely none of his business, but then thought better of it and said instead, 'I'll break it to him gently. We were never really an item, as such, but it's a long and complicated story and I won't bore you with it.'

I followed Stuart down the stairs in a very different frame of mind from when I had climbed them such a short time ago. I was elated, buzzing, and full of disbelief that this very nice-looking man thought me attractive and wanted to take me out. I was also full of the kind of lustful thoughts I hadn't had for a very, very long time.

On my way home from class the following night, I found myself making a detour and pulling up outside Owen's new home. It was an end of terrace – just as he had described – on a corner plot, so that it had a bigger garden than the neighbouring houses. There was a light on behind the closed curtains of the living room, so I locked the car, made my way up the path and rang the bell.

It was clear he was surprised, shocked even, to find me on the step. 'Evie,' he said, and looked as if he was waiting for me to bite his head off, as well he might.

'Sorry, it's so late. I thought we should talk, perhaps without raised voices for once.' I looked up at him. 'What's happened to us, Owen? It wasn't meant to be like this.'

His shoulders sagged, but there was such a look of relief on his face. 'I'm so pleased to see you, really I am. Will you come inside?'

I followed him into the house, and looked about me with interest, because having viewed the house with Owen I was quite keen to see what he had done with it. The answer was – absolutely nothing. I couldn't quite believe it, but it was painfully obvious that the furniture had been dumped haphazardly about the room and left surrounded by boxes that no apparent effort had been made to unpack.

Owen saw me looking and said defensively, 'Obviously I don't have your home-making skills.'

'I would have helped,' I pointed out. 'You only had to ask.'

He wandered through to the kitchen, which was in a similar state, put the kettle on and began to search for some clean cups. 'Hardly – I think you'd have told me where to get off – quite rightly,' he hastened to add, probably correctly interpreting the look I gave him, 'and I know that it's my fault, jumping in continually with my size tens. I really am sorry, Evie. I don't know what the hell's been the matter with me, behaving like an over-protective parent at best and a jealous lover at worst.'

'Well,' I said, considering, 'I suppose I could have been more forthcoming about the men frequenting my house – though you shouldn't have been so quick to jump to conclusions – and I really didn't see why I should *have* to explain anything to you. We *had* gone our separate ways and were never a real couple in the first place, despite the fact that we shared a house for so long.'

He hung his head and I noticed his normally close-cropped hair was over-long and really needed cutting; a closer look revealed that his overall appearance was quite scruffy. I actually couldn't believe the deterioration in him in such a short time. I wondered why the children hadn't mentioned it, but they were young, concerned with their own lives, and perhaps hadn't even noticed – or they thought I wouldn't care. I didn't like the feeling this last idea gave me, because I did care about Owen *and* the children, despite what Alice had said.

'I can pop round when I'm not teaching,' I offered. 'Give you a hand – as long as you don't think I'm interfering.'

'That would be gre—' he began, obviously about to accept my offer with alacrity, but then he hesitated, and eventually asked, 'but what about your writing?'

'I've not managed to get that organized,' I said ruefully, 'despite the posh office. I've only just got straight myself, and Christmas is only just around the corner.'

'Don't remind me.' Owen groaned. 'Do you have any plans?'

'We'll all have to get together at some point,' I supposed out loud, and then shook my head. 'But first things first, Owen. Let's get you sorted out and then we'll have a think about that. If your bedrooms are anything like this we need to get a move on, because you'll probably have at least two of the children staying with you for a night or two during the festivities. Have you eaten?'

He shook his head, which didn't surprise me at all.

'Pop and get yourself a take-away.' I indicated the various cartons and plastic containers littering the worktops, and said wryly, 'you must be on first-name terms with all of the local ones by the look of it. I'll make a start in here while you're gone.'

By the time he came back with a Chinese, which included some of my favourite dishes, I was touched to note, the kitchen at least was starting to look less as if it was waiting to be condemned by the health department and I was hungry enough to join Owen at the small table and tuck in.

Between us, after we'd eaten, we managed to arrange the sitting room furniture into some semblance of an order that made good use of the limited space and to pile the boxes into one corner out of the way for unpacking later. Already the place was starting to look more like a home and the awkwardness between us had thankfully been replaced with easy conversation and old jokes.

'I'll pop in when I get a minute, and carry on, if you don't mind me having a key, but,' I warned, 'once you're all straight, you're on your own, mind. You're not helpless, Owen, and when we lived together you were as good at keeping the place tidy as I was.'

'I know. I just couldn't seem to work up any enthusiasm on my own.'

'Tch, tch.' I clicked my tongue disapprovingly. 'Not good

enough – and Owen....' He looked up from investigating the contents of a large unlabelled box. 'get your hair cut. It's almost long enough to plait.'

We both started laughing at such a ridiculous statement and that started us reminiscing about the epidemic of head-lice that had seen us all infected and sitting round watching TV doused with evil-smelling treatments and feeling pretty sorry for ourselves.

'Do you remember, someone rang the doorbell and none of us would go and answer it?'

'Whoever it was must have known we were at home with every light on and the television blaring. It took ages for them to give up and go away. I think that was when I started keeping my hair short.' Owen ran a hand through his hair and it practically stood up in spikes. It wasn't normally long enough to do that. 'I'll get it cut tomorrow.'

'I could do it for you, but I doubt if we would find the box with the clippers in it any time soon.'

'No chance.' He smiled, and I thought he was already looking far more like his old self. 'And you've done quite enough for me for now. It's getting late. Thank you so much, Evie.'

'You're very welcome,' I told him, and I meant it.

I drove off with his key safely attached to my key ring and feeling really pleased that I had called round. That was when I realized I hadn't even mentioned the fact that I was going out on a date, despite the fact that it was the one reason I had gone to see him in the first place.

Seven

November rushed towards December and I did get some use out of my new office space by writing Christmas cards and wrapping presents up there. The big stationery cupboard that I'd had incorporated into the layout was an excellent storage place – especially as there was very little stationery in there, because despite my intention to visit Staples and stock up I had yet to make the trip.

My second date with Stuart loomed – which was a miracle in itself: I had very nearly cancelled the first one at the last minute because of a serious bout of self-doubt and extremely cold feet.

My biggest concern was, typically, what the hell was I going to wear? I didn't want to appear so casual that it looked as if I'd made no effort at all, but on the other hand I didn't want to go overboard and look as if I was going all-out to impress.

In the end I opted for a brand new pair of indigo skinny jeans, tucked into knee-high boots, and worn with a silky tunic top in black, grey and cream that skimmed my figure in a very advantageous way, with a three-quarter length black leather jacket over the top. It turned out to be a good choice for the relaxed evening we spent in a charming country pub, chatting as if we'd known each other for years, and afterwards we smooched outside my house in the car like a couple of teenagers. Watching Stuart drive away in his VW Passat with the windows all steamed up made me laugh out loud as I slid my key into the door.

I didn't have a lot of spare time, but with an hour here and there Owen's house soon began to look like the home it was meant to be. He thanked me effusively the few times he returned when I was still there, and bought me flowers – requesting me not to throw them at him this time – and some champagne to keep for Christmas. When I was done I tried to return his key.

'Keep it,' he urged. 'I'd like you to think of it as your second home.'

I didn't know how to insist that he should take it back without offending him, but I had no intention of returning the favour by passing over my own spare front door key, and seriously wished that I had just posted it through the letterbox. I still hadn't told him about Stuart – there just hadn't seemed to be the right moment – and I didn't want him walking in on us at my place and causing a scene.

It soon became apparent through various telephone conversations I had with the children that they were expecting us to all spend Christmas Day together as usual. I actually saw no harm in that. We were still a family, be it a rather unconventional one, and Christmas was about families. I even offered to do the cooking and host the meal, since it was either that or go to a restaurant, with Owen's house having no room for a decent-sized table that would seat us all. Christmas lunch eaten from a tray on our laps just didn't seem right somehow.

Between themselves the children had sorted out the logistics of the accommodation. Mai and Ella were to share my spare room, with Connor on a blow-up bed in my office. Unsurprisingly, Alice preferred to take advantage of Owen's hospitality and spare room, thereby relegating Jake to the use of his father's couch. I was supposing she would climb down from her high horse for long enough to join the rest of us for Christmas lunch at my place, but that was for her to decide.

My effort to do something good for the family almost caused my first argument with Stuart on what was only our second date. I hadn't thought to consult him first because it was only our second date, and the evening was almost spoiled before it had begun. The problem, as ever, had been trying to explain to Stuart what my exact relationship with Owen was and had been over the years we shared a home with each other and our children.

Stuart listened and made little comment – until I detailed my plans for a family Christmas Day.

'I had hoped we might be able to do something together.' He had looked disappointed and not a little a bit disgruntled.

'And we can,' I assured him. ''Just not on Christmas Day. I haven't been seeing you for much more than five minutes, so it's a bit soon to be introducing you to my children.'

'And it isn't just *your* children, is it? It all seems very odd to me, especially when most single parents manage to cope perfectly well. I'm not sure I can get my head round this *arrangement* of yours.'

I had already done my best to explain my previous living intricacies to him. I suppose in my heart I knew that being childless himself, he couldn't possibly truly understand the difficult situation we'd had found ourselves in or appreciate the vulnerability that had driven us together. At that time I had been recently deserted by an uncaring husband and Owen had just lost his young wife. To my mind, looking back, it was hardly surprising that we had been drawn together, but I supposed you would have to be in that position to really appreciate it.

For that reason I refused to be drawn into further detailed discussion; I just shrugged and stated briefly, 'Not many people can. Over the years we both got heartily sick of trying to clarify that our relationship wasn't what it seemed. I can only say that it suited Owen and me – and especially the children – and that we intend to stay friends even though we are going our separate ways.'

'He didn't seem very friendly when I saw him. Decidedly uncool about any of the male species being in your vicinity, I'd have said. I do find that odd behaviour in someone who just shared living space with you for convenience's sake. Does he know about us, Evie?'

'I didn't know there was an "us" he should know about, Stuart. Seeing each other on all of two occasions doesn't constitute an association of any great significance in my book,' I said, recognizing that I sounded a bit pompous but unable to think of any other way of putting it at that precise moment.

'But an association that has lasted fifteen years – even though it isn't a "relationship" – does?' he queried, with a straight look.

'I seem to remember that you're divorced,' I said pointedly. 'How long did you say you were married?'

'Ah, but that ended acrimoniously. I told you, she didn't like the long hours I worked building up the business. She found someone with more time on his hands. *We* broke up – you two didn't.'

This was just the kind of conversation I didn't want to be having and I was regretting my effort to be honest, just as I always had in the past, but I really liked Stuart, so I had to keep trying.

'The arrangement between Owen and me came to a natural conclusion as soon as the last child left home. I'm glad, for the children's sake and for ours, that it wasn't an acrimonious split because they can still share their free time between us without feeling guilty. Between us we're still the only parents those children have, and that makes us a family. I'm not going to pretend otherwise or fall out with Owen just to make you feel better. Yes, recently, he's behaved like an idiot – something he freely admits – but everything is fine now and it makes life easier all round if we can be the good friends we always have been.'

'So you'll tell him about us,' he persisted.

'Yes.' I nodded. 'When, and if, there is something to tell.'

'I hope there will be.' He smiled suddenly, explaining ruefully, 'I'm not usually this insecure, but I can't imagine living in the same house as you for fifteen days – never mind fifteen years – and not hoping for much more than friendship.'

'Flatterer.' I couldn't help laughing but there was no mistaking the clear look of desire in his eyes and I shivered, too, especially when he leaned across the table between us and captured my lips for a brief moment with his own. From then on we had a really lovely time and Owen wasn't mentioned again.

For this second date Stuart had booked a table at Annabelle's after discovering that it was one of my favourite restaurants. On reflection I hoped he realized it was because of the fabulous menu and didn't think it was just because I favoured the booths taking up the centre of the room. The high sides afforded the diners a privacy that was quite unique in an eatery and I wondered how Stuart had managed to secure one, because they were very popular indeed and diners booked well in advance.

Knowing the venue we would be heading for had been an advantage, and I had pushed out the boat and purchased a whole new outfit. With all the upheaval of moving my weight was less than it had been for quite some time, so I treated myself to a figure-hugging top and pencil skirt, both in black, with matching tights and a very pointed pair of killer heels that I would never have tried either to drive or to walk far in. The jacket, I thought, made the outfit, being in an eye-catching black-and-white zebra print and very close-fitted. I knew I was looking good – and I didn't think to add the rider 'for my age', not even in my own mind.

I was glad I'd made the effort when I opened the front door

earlier to my tall, dark and handsome escort who was clad, in what I recognized as an Armani suit in black, with a crisp white shirt, and a red tie adding a splash of colour. He looked good enough to eat and I was glad I was ready to leave, because I feared the consequences of letting him inside my door, especially when he looked me up and down and said, 'You look absolutely gorgeous,' and sounded as if he really meant it..

Once the touchy subject of Owen and my previous living arrangements – which had quite spoiled the first course – had been dropped, the intimacy between us built deliciously as we tasted food from each other's forks and our legs nudged under the table. I realized that I hadn't felt like this about anyone since Kevin, and the sudden and unwelcome thought of my ex-husband suddenly made me understandably wary and determined not to rush into anything with Stuart.

There was no doubting the sexual attraction between us – the air was practically crackling every time we touched – but at my age I didn't want to be leaping into bed with someone I scarcely knew. In fact, I wouldn't have wanted that at any age.

This time, at the end of the evening, he leapt out of the car as soon as we drew up outside my house, opening my door for me and walking me up the path to the front door. There was no doubt in my mind that he was expecting to be invited in – especially as our kisses became increasingly ardent.

'Aren't you going to ask me in?' Stuart asked eventually, when the invitation wasn't forthcoming, his breathing was ragged, his look hot, heavy and longing.

I successfully fought the desire to just give in and enjoy the delights he would undoubtedly have to offer. Ruthlessly ignoring the voice that reminded me it had been a very long time and I was of an age to please myself, wasn't easy – not to the mention the clamouring of my eager body, but I shook my head reluctantly.

I guessed women rarely rejected his advances and I was in no doubt of his state of arousal, but he merely said softly, 'Are you sure?'

'I'm sure.'

I was certain he would try to persuade me to change my mind, or even get annoyed, and was relieved when he did neither, but just wrapped me tightly in his arms and kissed all the breath out of me before letting me go. He held me at arm's length before drawing me closer again, looking down at me for a very long moment before kissing me briefly once more, then walking away.

He was absolutely gorgeous. What the hell was I thinking? Why couldn't I just take what he offered for however long it lasted and just enjoy it for what it was? I would probably never hear from him again now and would spend the rest of my life wondering what I had missed.

I had turned away and was fumbling for my key when he called, 'Good night, Evie. I really enjoyed tonight. I'll call you tomorrow,' before driving off. Having opened the door at last I skipped inside with the biggest smile on my face, floated off to bed and slept dreamlessly through the night.

True to his promise, Stuart did ring the next day, though it didn't look as if we would be meeting any time soon. He had already said the orders had been building up, with everyone predictably wanting their office, kitchen or bedroom fitted before Christmas.

'We're going to be working late through the week and probably even weekends to keep on top of it,' he explained, and I had no reason to disbelieve him. If I had visitors coming to share the festivities and the house was in uproar, I would want the work completed, too.

'Honestly, don't worry,' I assured him. 'I'll have enough to do with winding up classes for the end of term and getting on top of the present – and food shopping for Christmas. I ought to spend some time with Arthur, too, because I've been neglecting him lately.'

'I'm not sure I like having a rival,' Stuart said with a laugh. His tone was carefully light, but I think we both knew that it wasn't actually Arthur he was referring to.

I was quite certain he would not have been the slightest bit impressed had he known that it was Owen who eventually turned up on my step with a Christmas tree and stayed on to help me put the decorations up.

I was just thankful to have someone who knew what they were doing, to untangle the tree lights and fix them when they fused and – if I was being totally truthful – it was lovely to have someone to share the memories of Christmases past. We reminisced over each tree decoration, the majority of them made or purchased by the children and amassed over many years. Not many would understand the value of a robin with a broken beak or a glass angel with only one wing.

The tree was far too big, clearly having been bought with the dimensions of a much bigger house in mind, and when

Owen had first arrived and realized this his dismay was clear to see.

'I'm so sorry, I just wasn't thinking.'

'It doesn't have to go in the hall,' I reminded him, though that was where it had always proudly stood in the old house.

'In fact,' he said ruefully, 'if you put it there, no one will be able to get in the door.'

'What about the corner of the dining room,' I suggested, and it was perfect once we had done a bit of judicious pruning and shuffled the furniture round a bit.

We stood back to admire it once all the decorations that had once adorned the untrimmed trees in much a bigger house had been determinedly yet artistically forced into place. There was no doubt it was overloaded, but then our Christmas trees always had been; it was the way we all liked to see them.

'Perfect,' Owen gave his nod of approval, 'and the fairy on the top hasn't even noticed that she's sitting a bit lower because we had to cut the top off.'

'I'm sure she was never fond of having that spike thrust up her skirt anyway. She looks much happier.'

We laughed uproariously, like naughty children at a smutty joke, and then enjoyed a sip or two more of mulled wine and nibbled hot mince pies before we set to work with the rest of the decorations. With the Christmas songs album playing in the background the house was beginning to feel very festive and very much like home.

'What about your house?' I suddenly turned from where I was standing on a chair pinning up a Merry Christmas banner that had seen better days, but still looked pretty as long as the main light wasn't on. 'There's nothing left for your tree and now we're using all of this stuff as well.'

Owen didn't look up from arranging Nativity figures in the crude stable that Jake had made in woodwork class at secondary school. 'I didn't think I'd bother,' he said.

I almost drove a pin into my finger. 'Oh, don't say that. It sounds so sad and now I feel mean for stealing Christmas from you.'

'We'll be here anyway,' he pointed out mildly.

'But only for Christmas Day.' I felt like crying. 'You know we always decorate early in December, or you wouldn't be here with the tree.' He went to speak, but I held up my hand. 'No, I'm not having it. I'm going out tomorrow to buy Christmas for your house and I'll be over to help you decorate.'

He came to lift me down and I hugged him. 'Can't have you without a Christmas, can we?'

Then we stood like that with our arms around each other admiring our handiwork, just as we had done on fifteen other Christmases. Except this one was very different and that was brought home when the doorbell rang and we sprang apart guiltily – or perhaps that was just me.

Eight

My relief at finding Arthur on the step almost overwhelmed me and I was probably over-effusive in my welcome because of that.

'Arthur,' I cried, 'and Gizmo, too. Come on in out of the cold.'

I was trying to pretend it didn't matter a jot to me exactly who had been standing on the step, but I wasn't fooling myself for a minute. Had it been Stuart, I would have, far more reluctantly, had to issue a similar invitation and then watch the expression on his face change from pleasure to deep suspicion as he'd taken in the festive and very cosy scene with Owen in the centre of it.

'Look, it's Arthur from next door and his dog, Gizmo,' I repeated for Owen's benefit, because somehow I didn't think they had ever been formally introduced, what with Owen storming off so regularly those first few days after I'd moved in.

Owen thrust out a hand, 'Lovely to meet you, Arthur. I'm Owen.' The two men shook hands, then Owen hunkered down and held out a hand tentatively to Gizmo. 'What a grand little chap,' he said, as Gizmo licked his fingers.

'He belonged to my late wife. She thought the world of him.'

'You're a widower then, like me. I expect you miss her.'

'Only every day,' Arthur said, adding without a trace of self-pity, 'but you have to get on with it, don't you? We're not here to mope. We had a good long marriage and our son was grown up with children of his own before she passed. I believe your children were quite young when you lost your wife and that must have been hard.'

I poured Arthur a mulled wine, put a mince pie onto a plate and watched as they sat down to chat.

'Pretty well impossible, until Evie and I got together, but it wasn't...'

'What it seemed,' Arthur finished the sentence for him and nodded his understanding. 'I know, Evie's told me all about it. What a blessing for you both, and for your children, that you had the good sense to see the benefits of getting together.'

'Mulled wine, Arthur, and a mince pie?' I brought them to the table and placed them in front of him, adding, 'Something of a tradition when we put the decorations up.'

Arthur raised his glass, 'I'll drink to tradition,' he said and, looking round, he nodded. 'It's looking grand.'

'Not too much?' I asked.

We all looked at the over-decorated tree and the dining and sitting rooms generously festooned with garlands; even the kitchen had a couple of bells hanging from the ceiling.

'You can never overdo Christmas,' Arthur stated, beaming

at us both. 'I can still mind our family Christmases, and the memories always make me smile.'

'Why don't you join us for ours?' Owen said suddenly, then as an afterthought he added, 'That's if Evie doesn't mind.'

'Owen took the words out of my mouth,' I insisted, and actually he had. 'Having you here for Christmas Day would make our day.'

Arthur didn't take too much persuading. He never did say what he'd come round for, though I thought that perhaps he'd heard the Christmas songs from his back garden when he let Gizzie out, and really wanted to be a part of whatever was going on.

'You didn't mind, did you?' Owen asked, when Arthur had returned to his own home. 'When I thought of him spending the day on his own I forgot it wasn't my place to issue invitations.'

'You only just beat me to it, Owen,' I reminded him. 'Having him here will be quite nice, won't it? The kids all missed out on having a grandparent, what with Kevin's parents making themselves scarce as soon as he did, mine being already settled in Australia, yours being that much older and living in Scotland, and Susan losing both of hers long before your children were even born.'

'There's no doubt they've been deprived, and therefore will probably adopt Arthur on the spot,' Owen was smiling. 'Now, about the food – I do want to pay my share.'

'And so you shall.'

'Do you want me to come to the supermarket with you?'

'But you hate supermarket shopping,' I reminded him, and watched his face fall. 'Well, we'll see,' I promised, but I determined not to accept his offer because, nice as this evening had been, everything was beginning to slip back into being exactly as it always had been. I didn't want to give the impression that nothing had changed – because everything had and it couldn't change back just because it was Christmas.

In the end it was Stuart who came to the supermarket with me, simply because he turned up his way home from a job on the off-chance we could spend an hour or two together, just as I was setting off.

'I can leave it,' I said immediately, thrilled to see him.

'I'll come with you,' he offered, just as quickly. 'It will be a whole new experience for me. Shopping for Christmas groceries for a family must be very different from shopping for one or two. In fact,' he said flatly, 'Claire and I always went away – usually skiing. The snow made it seem a bit more festive than a beach in Barbados might have done.'

'Mmm, skiing wouldn't tempt me, at Christmas or any other time of the year, but a beach in Barbados holds definite attractions for me,' I mused dreamily. Since the Beetle wasn't known for its roomy boot, I happily accepted his offer to drive and hopped nimbly into his work van.

'We could do that,' he said, concentrating on pulling out of the close and not looking at me. 'You know, holiday in Barbados – after Christmas, of course.'

'Really?' I stared at him, because it sounded as if he was envisaging a future together for us – even if it was only the immediate future.

'Why not?' Stuart did look at me then, with a raised eyebrow.

I said the first thing that came into my head, and it was practical, at least. 'It would have to be half-term because of my classes.'

'When's that?'

'Mid-February.'

'It will still be hot in Barbados then,' he said knowledge-ably, making me laugh, and adding lightly, 'February it is then.'

He carried on making me laugh all around the store, taking charge of the trolley and forcing it to go straight in spite of the wonky wheel, and seriously discussing the merits of homemade versus packet stuffing, and turkey opposed to goose, when it was perfectly clear he didn't have a single clue what the hell he was talking about. We must have been an hour deciding which crackers had the most to offer in the way of attractive presentation, hat, motto and novelty.

I only just stopped myself from saying that Owen was the only one in the family who still put a paper hat on, and pointed out instead that the novelties always ended up in the bin.

'Ah,' he said, holding up a very fancy box, 'but they wouldn't if they were worth having, *and*,' he said, as if it clinched the matter, 'you'll get a much better class of motto with these. I can practically guarantee they won't end up in the bin.'

It was as if thinking of Owen had somehow conjured him up in person because as we headed, still laughing our heads off, towards the delicatessen we bumped smack into him. The expression on his face as he took in the picture of us together pushing the family Christmas in the trolley almost tore my heart out.

If I'd given the matter any thought at all, I would have said the chance of meeting him was exceedingly slim, but in a small town like Brankstone there was only one major supermarket within a reasonable distance, so there always was a chance.

'Glad to see you found someone willing to help you bring the Christmas feast home,' he joked, as soon as he'd collected himself, 'though I did offer.'

Stuart obviously took in the situation at a glance and he really surprised me by immediately pouring oil on what could have been troubled waters by saying, 'Oh, I just turned up at an opportune moment and immediately got roped in.'

'I expect you'll be joining us, then, on Christmas Day. Least you deserve, I'd say.' Owen sounded most civilized. Only I could have guessed the effort it took him to issue such an invitation when it was obviously the very last thing he wanted.

'Evie's already told me it's a bit soon to include me and I'd already made my own plans anyway – nice of you to offer, though.'

'Stuart and I have only recently started seeing each other.' I was so glad of the opportunity to make that clear. 'I think this constitutes our third date.'

'See what happens when I let her choose the venue,' Stuart complained and we all managed to laugh.

'Well, nice to meet you, Stuart.' Owen held out a hand and they shook. 'Let me know what I owe you, Evie.' He indicated the contents of his own trolley which comprised a variety of meals for one. 'My bill should be quite a bit lower.'

'About the same as mine usually is by the look of it.' Stuart nodded, before adding, 'It seems we have the same taste.' He didn't need to look at me for his meaning to be clear.

I felt a bit shaky, but I couldn't have said why. It wasn't as if I was doing anything wrong. To hide my confusion I made a big show of selecting cheeses, giving the choices all of my attention.

'Well,' said Stuart, as we walked away with a selection that included everyone's particular favourite, 'that could have been awkward. He obviously didn't have a clue we were seeing each other. When were you going to tell him?'

I stopped in the middle of the aisle and gave him a straight look. 'As I've already told you – I was going to tell Owen and the children when I was quite certain there was something to tell,' I said firmly.

'You don't think that I'm serious about you, do you, Evie?'

'I really have no idea,' I found myself saying honestly but, before he could reply, someone requested, 'Excuse us, please.'

Steering the trolley out of the way I turned to make my apology to the couple waiting to pass. 'Oh, I'm so sor—'

'Evie? It *is* you,' the woman said. 'I wasn't quite sure from the back.'

'Sandy – and James, too – this is a pleasant surprise.'

There were a lot of exclamations, hugging, and explanations of their being in the area to visit relatives before I remembered Stuart, waiting patiently by the trolley.

'Oh, I'm sorry.' I hurried to introduce him a little awkwardly. 'This is Stuart, my – ah – friend.'

While Stuart and James were shaking hands Sandy took the opportunity to waggle her eyebrows about and look him up and down in what she obviously fondly assumed to be an approving way.

When it was her turn she said, in the most exaggerated way, 'So pleased to meet you, Stuart. I'd like to say I've heard all about you, but Evie has obviously been keeping your existence all to herself or I'd have heard about you through the Brankstone grapevine.'

Even I laughed. 'We've been seeing each other all of five minutes, Sandy, and I've been busy moving house.'

'Oh, yes,' James put in, 'we got your change of address card. Finally got the children off your hands and moved on after – how long was it? – Fifteen years?'

'We never thought it would happen,' Sandy said, shaking her head, 'you and Owen going your separate ways, did we, James? We could have sworn you would end up together for real.'

She was beginning to get on my nerves and I thought her extremely tactless in discussing my liaison with Owen – or lack of one – in front of Stuart, so I said flatly, 'It wasn't going to happen. Sandy. You of all people should know that.'

'I suppose so, but it seemed such a shame. We introduced them, you know,' she informed Stuart, 'thinking they would be the ideal couple, but the relationship never was...'

'...what it seemed,' Stuart finished for her. 'I know, but I'm hoping ours will eventually be *exactly* what it seems.'

It was such a lovely thing to say, and I think I started to fall in love with him a little then. I still breathed a sigh of relief when we managed to get away, though, after making promises that I didn't intend to keep to meet up while Sandy and James were in the area.

'I must apologize for Sandy.' I pulled a face.

'Don't,' he said, putting his hand over mine on the trolley handle. 'If I was still harbouring any doubts about the role Owen played in your life for such a long time, she has managed to abolish them completely. I should be thanking her.'

I felt I should have been cross that he had obviously still had his doubts, but I'd have to be the first to agree that our circumstances had been unusual, to say the least. I was also thrilled by what Stuart had said about his hopes for us.

We finished the rest of the shopping without further interruption, Stuart proved to be a master at packing, and in no time I had paid an eye-watering amount to the cashier and we were making for the exit.

'I've never seen anything like it,' Owen commented, when we finally arrived home and had hauled everything into the house, 'the food and the decorations.'

'You think it's a bit over the top?' I tried not to sound defensive. 'Well, maybe it is, but that first year in the same house I think we both tried to over-compensate because of the missing parent in each family – and it's kind of stuck.'

'But the children are adults now,' he pointed out.

'Didn't you have traditions?'

'Only the skiing – but I suppose it's different when you have kids.'

'It is,' I agreed. 'Even when they're grown up.'

'I'd like to meet your children,' Stuart said suddenly.

'And so you shall,' I promised, from the depths of a

cupboard where I was organizing the tins; then, surfacing, I added, 'but it will have to be all five of them together – Owen's as well. I'll tell them about you when they are all at home for the holiday. It will make things easier.'

'Easier?'

'If I tell one on the phone the first one will be sharing the news with the others before I replace the receiver. I want them all to hear it from me – otherwise you will seem like a guilty secret.'

'And I'm not?'

'No reason for me to feel guilty – or to keep you a secret.' I spoke emphatically, and I believed it, but that didn't stop me wondering what the reaction was going to be.

Nine

I don't know how I did it in the time, but by the week before Christmas everything was just about organized and even the cards had been posted. Somehow, I had also managed to find the time to make Owen's tiny sitting room look festive with garlands and holly, though I cheated with the tree and plumped for a fibre optic one. At the last minute I also bought a smaller one for Arthur. His face was an absolute picture when I'd set it up and flicked the switch.

'I'd no idea they had such things.' He stared at it, scratching his thinning curls in amazement.

'You don't like it,' I stated, disappointed but accepting that his taste would obviously run to the more traditional.

'Oh I do, Evie,' he assured me. 'How on earth does the whole tree change colour like that? It's an absolute picture and I shall waste hours just looking at it. Wait until I tell our Ron about it.'

I smiled, pleased with the way the pretty tree made the room immediately seem more festive.

'Our children will start arriving from tomorrow,' I said,

realizing how much I was looking forward to seeing them for more than a few hours. 'They've all managed to get Christmas off, which is pretty amazing, though some will be arriving earlier and others probably leaving later. For the bit in the middle, in particular Christmas Day, we'll all be together, which is the important thing.'

'Are you sure we won't be imposing, Gizmo and me? Christmas is a family time.'

'Isn't there a saying along the lines of friends being the family that you choose for yourself?' I asked, 'and anyway, I think Owen and I have managed to prove without a doubt that you don't have to *be* family to *become* a family, don't you?'

'True.' Arthur beamed.

Wishing to be neighbourly, and with Arthur's invaluable help over the names, I wrote a Christmas card for each person living in the close, with an invitation enclosed in the envelopes requesting them to join us for mulled wine and nibbles on Christmas Eve.

'I wouldn't get your hopes up,' he warned, 'because they do seem to prefer to keep themselves to themselves. The neighbours in the close were much friendlier in years gone by, but in recent times Win was the only one I ever managed to become good friends with – and now you.'

'Really?' I felt quite disappointed, but had to admit that friendly greetings were definitely few and far between whenever I ventured out, and those were more likely to come from the postman, milkman and paperboy than the other residents. Still, it was Christmas and I felt I should at least make the effort.

'Oh, I don't think so, dear,' was my first response from the elderly lady three doors along, and, 'thenk you, but mey husband and ay are fa-ar too busy,' came from the exceedingly snobbish female half of the couple Arthur had mentioned on my other side. I immediately decided that I didn't want her looking down her long nose at either my Christmas decorations or my family. I could just imagine her reaction should she learn of our circumstances. No one else even bothered to respond. Well, I had been warned by Arthur and should have expected it, I supposed.

For perhaps the first time I began to miss my old multicultural neighbourhood full of working parents and commuters who were never too busy to pass the time of day and accepted everyone at face value.

I felt I had reason to be pleased when a meeting at the school the following evening culminated in a festive get-together of tutors and admin staff. At least that went some way towards making up for my unsociable neighbours.

In the end the party went on for longer than I had anticipated but I really enjoyed it and made arrangements to meet up with the people I was particularly friendly with in the New Year. It was time to get my social life back on track, I decided, now that things were settling down.

I arrived home in a good mood to a note on my doormat informing me that Mai and Ella had arrived and were waiting next door. I didn't have to think too hard about which next door was referred to and hastened to tap on Arthur's door.

The girls abandoned their mugs of hot chocolate temporarily to wrap me in warm hugs when I followed

Arthur inside, and assured me they had been very well looked after in my absence; and they followed that up with the demand to know why they had never been allowed to have a sweet little dog like Gizmo when they were all growing up.

'Erm, because it was left to me to look after the rabbit, the fish, the gerbils, and all manner of other sundry animals,' I reminded them, laughing, and Arthur was quick to join in with similar memories of the pets Ron had been allowed to own and then had not taken care of. I shuddered and accepted that I had actually got off lightly when he mentioned a snake.

I was loath to hurry them away, since they were clearly all enjoying each other's company and it was quite late by the time we eventually made it indoors with the heavy holdalls that the girls assured me were stuffed with Christmas presents.

'No dirty washing then?' I said, dumping the bag I was hefting into the spare room. 'That's a relief.'

'We-ell,' Mai said, with a cheeky smile, 'there may be just a couple of things.'

'And a couple among my things, too,' Ella admitted, 'like the top I want to wear on Christmas Day, my favourite jeans and—'

'Stop,' I held up my hand, 'I get the picture.'

We all looked at each other and burst out laughing, happy to be together and already getting into the usual banter.

Mai was my daughter, eighteen years old, slim and blonde, and Ella was Owen's nineteen-year-old daughter, also slim and blonde. They could have been mistaken for twins – and often were. Only three and four years old when Owen and I cobbled our families together, they had bonded immediately and been inseparable ever since.

Studying at different universities didn't seem to have affected their close relationship in the slightest. However, I could only guess at the phone bills they must have been running up between them and made a mental note to get Owen to check that they were on the best mobile contracts for their usage. Watching them settle in to the twin bedded room, talking nineteen to the dozen, it seemed as if they'd never been apart and little had really changed apart from the accommodation. I found myself wishing, rather futilely, that Alice could have been as accepting.

How different it was next morning for me to wake to the sound of bright chatter from the two girls, already up and pottering in the kitchen by the sound of it. I was proved right when my bedroom door inched open and two smiling faces – one above the other – peered in.

'Good morning.' I couldn't keep the huge smile from my face, finally admitting to myself how much I had missed having the family around me and becoming even more determined to enjoy every minute of the time they were here.

'You're awake.' Mai was first through the door with a cup of tea, closely followed by Ella with two slices of toast on a plate.

'What would you have done if I'd been asleep?' I asked, biting into hot toast liberally spread with butter.

'The same as we've been doing for the past hour,' Ella said cheekily. 'Just keep boiling the kettle and toasting the bread until you woke up. I'm afraid we've used almost a whole loaf of bread.'

'Good grief,' I said.

'We didn't waste any,' Mai assured me, 'because we ate most of it ourselves and even took some round to Arthur.'

I almost choked on my tea. 'Good grief,' I said again.

By the time I had enjoyed the luxury of breakfast in bed, and a long leisurely shower, coffee was waiting for me in a kitchen that had been cleared of all signs of breakfast. While dressing I had been treated to the sound of the vacuum cleaner being vigorously applied to carpet and as I sipped my coffee I could see through the window that washing was already pegged on the line and blowing well in a brisk December breeze.

'You have been busy,' I approved, taking my drink to sit at the dining table where they both joined me.

'So have you,' Ella said, setting the biscuit barrel down. 'The tree looks gorgeous.'

'Thank you. I have to confess that your dad helped, quite a lot in fact, especially with the lights, so if you'd said it looked terrible I would have advised you to blame him.'

'It was nice of you to find the time to decorate Owen's house as well,' Mai said, turning over the contents of the barrel, looking for one of her favourite custard creams; passing Ella a bourbon cream she came across she added, 'You've been really busy. Is there anything that we can do to help?'

I watched fondly as the two of them devoured biscuits one after the other and marvelled at where they were putting them – and after all that toast, too.

'No, everything is under control, just the turkey to collect – a fresh one of course. Are you two getting enough to eat?'

They looked at each other and then at the depleted biscuit supply and giggled.

'Lots of beans on toast and pot noodles, but the NHS bursary won't run to biscuits.' Mai went to put the lid back on the barrel, and I stopped her, saying, 'Eat up, both of you. I don't grudge you anything and certainly not a measly packet of biscuits or three – though,' I continued, 'I'll keep the fancy Christmas ones hidden for now, if it's all the same to you.' I watched their eyes light up.

It was lovely to enjoy their cheerful company and, with no teaching until the new term in January and the preparations for Christmas all in hand, I was free to do just that. We made mince pies, just as we used to do when they were small children, and then, while the pies were in the oven, we went upstairs with a quilt, pillows and bedding, inflated the blow-up bed for Connor and made it up.

'It's a lovely work space.' Ella looked around enviously, 'and I have an assignment to complete before I go back to university after Christmas. Do you think...?'

'Of course,' I agreed immediately. 'Someone had best make use of it, because so far I've only written Christmas cards and replied to emails up here.'

'Mu-um,' Mai tried to sound disapproving and stern, but didn't quite bring it off, 'what about the novel you were going to write once you had your office?'

'Still up here.' I tapped my head and explained. 'What with moving and Christmas there's just been too much going on for me to do much more than think about it.'

I caught a look between them but couldn't quite interpret its meaning, so I just continued, 'Plenty of time when the festivities are over. January and February are dreary months, anyway. That's the ideal time to be snug indoors, I'll make a start then. Actually,' I said, more as a distraction than anything else, 'you can both help to carry the presents down and put them under the tree. They're in that cupboard. And,' I went on as they fell over each other to get there first, 'no feeling and trying to guess the contents or it will spoil the surprise.'

I was wasting my breath, and I knew it, as I watched them almost wrench the door from its hinges and began to ooh and aah over the brightly wrapped parcels.

We were loaded up when the doorbell rang and we all tried to get down the stairs first, guessing it heralded the arrival of Connor.

'You didn't have to go to all this trouble.' He beamed, taking in the three of us weighed down with gifts. 'They're all for me, I take it?'

Somehow we hugged and kissed around our burdens, then he said appreciatively, 'Something smells good,' and we ran shrieking to rescue the mince pies from the oven, with Connor following more slowly and laughing loudly.

'Nothing much seems to have changed – except you're in a different kitchen,' he commented, watching the three of us tripping over each other to take pies from the oven and lift them from the tins on to wire cooling trays. 'Haven't any of you ever heard the saying that too many cooks spoil the broth?'

'Be quiet, smart arse,' commented Ella cheerfully. 'Just try one of these and see what you think.'

We all watched him anxiously as we waited for the verdict, and he took his time delivering it. First admiring the pie from all angles – while transferring it from hand to hand because it was still hot enough to burn his fingers – eventually he took a bite and we each held our breath while he chewed slowly and ponderously, apparently savouring the texture and the flavour before he bit into it again and began to repeat the process.

In the end Mai lost patience with him. 'Oh, get on with it, Connor, do. You're not on *Come Dine With Me*, you know.'

Refusing to be hurried, he carried on eating slowly and then, when he had swallowed the last mouthful, said, 'I believe I would need to test another before being able to give an honest opinion.' With that he snatched another from the cooling tray and ran off, laughing and spraying crumbs everywhere, with the girls in hot pursuit.

'OK, OK, I give in,' he yelled when he was finally pinned down with the girls on top of him. 'They're perfect.'

'Jeez,' Ella said, getting up and dusting off her hands as if she had just beaten him in some sort of tournament. 'All that just to get him to state the obvious. I really do hope he never applies to be a judge on *Ready, Steady Cook*.'

By this time I was laughing so hard that I had to hold onto the worktop because I was in real danger of collapsing. 'Stop now, that's enough,' I pleaded. 'Girls, the parcels won't put themselves under the tree.' I indicated the pile we had abandoned in the middle of the dining room table while we rescued the pies from the oven. 'And, Connor, you're in my office on a blow-up bed, so if you'd like to bring your bags in…?' I've put a clothes' rail up there for you.'

Mai looked up from where she was artistically arranging presents in a circle under the tree. 'You are joking,' she scoffed. 'I don't think he ever familiarized himself with coat hangers. He always hung most of his clothes on the floor – and he probably still does.'

'Well, I won't even dignify those remarks with a response,' said Connor, and lifting his nose snootily in the air he made for the door, where he paused to ask, 'Is it all right to park in the close, because I saw a net curtain or two twitching in what I took to be disapproval?'

'They don't seem to be the friendliest of neighbours,' I said regretfully, 'but as long as you're not over anyone's driveway, I don't think they can have anything to say. Your car will easily fit in alongside mine at the front, though, so put it there.'

'*We* decided to come by train using our student passes,' said Ella in a superior tone, standing back to admire the effect of the prettily arranged packages. 'Less trouble all round.'

'And if you wanted to go into town for any reason while you were here you would rely on public transport, of course. So, I wouldn't need to offer anyone a lift – not even if they missed the last bus home.' Connor said all of this in such a reasonable tone that I hid a smile and watched as Ella hesitated.

'We—ell,' she said at last, 'when you put it like that, you are, of course, the kindest, most generous of brothers.'

I loved it when the children talked like that, easily dismissing the fact that they weren't actually blood relatives; Connor being my son, and Ella Owen's daughter. It always made me feel a bit emotional, if I was being honest.

Blinking quickly, I encouraged, 'Bring the car in and get your stuff upstairs, then you can all decide what you would like for dinner, while I make sandwiches for lunch.'

'Shepherd's pie,' they all yelled in unison without even a pause for thought.

'Well, that's really going to stretch my culinary talents,' I said. 'I don't know why I even bothered to ask for a preference when I already knew the answer. We could invite Arthur, he'd love that. Did I tell you he's going to join us on Christmas Day?'

'Lovely,' Ella said, then she hesitated and there was a moment of uncomfortable silence before she asked, 'And your new man – will he be joining us, too?'

Ten

The words, 'your new man,' seemed to ring out with startling clarity and all movement was suddenly suspended. As if I was standing outside myself, I watched us all cease in our actions with one accord, to become as still as statues in a weirdly silent tableau.

I'd been caught in the act of buttering bread and froze on the spot with the knife loaded with butter and poised ready to spread. Connor had stopped halfway through the door and was obviously uncertain whether to continue forward, or come back into the room, and Mai sat up so suddenly that she knocked a plastic reindeer off the tree and had pine needles in her hair.

'Oh, Ella,' she said eventually in a reproving voice, 'you know we agreed not to say anything.'

'I know,' Ella hung her head, 'but it just kind of – slipped out. I'm sorry, Evie, I know it isn't any of our business who you see but I didn't want you to think we disapproved, either.'

I managed to raise a smile from somewhere and assured her, 'It's fine Ella, really it is, and of course it's your business

– more than anybody else's – but I was waiting to talk to you about it when you were all together. Who told you? Not your dad?'

I didn't think I would ever be able to forgive Owen if it had been him. He would know, of all people, that I would want to talk to the children myself about any developments in my private life and would surely have respected that.

I didn't realize I was holding my breath until Ella said, 'No, it wasn't Dad, though he obviously knows if you're asking that.'

'Only very recently, and only because he bumped into us. Look, let's sit down and we can talk about it properly. Not that there's much to talk about yet,' I assured them as we moved to the sitting room end of the room and seated ourselves on the couches there.

'The point is that my dating anyone is only very recent indeed. You must know I haven't been involved with anybody in any serious way for several years. As it is, I've seen Stuart all of three times, so you can hardly call it a meaningful relationship and – to answer your question, Ella – no, he will not be joining us for Christmas Day. It will just be family – and Arthur,' I added, 'but I didn't think you would mind that. May I ask who did tell you, if it wasn't your dad?'

'It was your old friend Sandy apparently,' Connor said. 'She told Alice when she called round to Owen's with a Christmas card and Alice immediately phoned the rest of us.' He looked to the girls for confirmation and they nodded.

I could feel the colour draining from my face. Alice – of all people – being told that I was seeing someone by anyone other than myself was the worst possible news.

I recognized Mai's 'She wasn't very pleased', for the massive understatement it was, and was amazed that Alice wasn't already round here, spitting her fury into my face.

'We tried to tell her it wasn't anything to do with us and you were a free agent,' Ella said, 'but you know what she's like.'

'Leave her to Jake and Owen,' Connor advised, 'they'll talk some sense into her.'

'But you don't understand how bad things are between us.' I was almost in tears and beginning to wish I had never met Stuart. If only he hadn't turned up just as I was about to go grocery shopping none of this would have happened, I thought with great futility. 'She blames me for breaking the family up.'

'Well, that's bloody well the most ridiculous bloody thing I ever heard,' Ella fumed, and I didn't even bother to tell her to stop swearing because I could tell how riled up she was. 'You, of all people, kept us together through all the years of us growing up. I don't know what she's thinking, to blame you for something we all grew up knowing perfectly well was going to happen one day.'

'She's just upset.' I felt I had to defend her.

'Upset that, after years of putting us first, you have the temerity to want a life of your own?' Connor, who was usually so mild, was starting to sound outraged himself. 'That girl needs to get over herself and realize everything isn't always about her.'

'Yes, Connor's right, Mum, and I did try to tell her that she has her own life and you are entitled to have yours,' Mai said.

'What did she say?' I asked.

'Nothing.' Mai grimaced. 'She hung up on me.'

'Perhaps I should go and try to talk to her,' I suggested, but nobody ventured to agree that that might be even a remotely good idea.

'You'll just get into a row,' said Ella, 'and, to be honest, I don't think you should feel obliged to justify yourself. She wouldn't if the boot were on the other foot.'

'That's absolutely right,' Mai agreed. 'Please or offend, Alice always does exactly what she wants to do and she wouldn't dream of consulting any of us.'

'Like I said before,' Connor chipped in, 'leave it to Jake and Owen. They know how to handle Alice.'

'I just don't want Christmas to be spoiled,' I fretted. 'What if she refuses to come here on Christmas Day?'

'Her loss,' Connor said flatly, and went to move his car.

'Her loss is right.' Ella nodded and, making her way back to the kitchen, said, 'Do you want me to finish doing the sandwiches, or shall I make a start on peeling the potatoes for the shepherd's pie?'

'I think,' Mai said, probably wisely I thought, 'that Alice needs to learn that the whole world doesn't actually revolve around Alice and what she wants. She is a grown woman and also a social worker, for God's sake. You would think that she'd seen all the hardships that life has to offer in her line of work and count herself lucky that we had such a normal and secure upbringing. Now,' she said briskly, 'can we talk about something other than Alice, please?'

In fact, the rest of the day passed very pleasantly indeed, as the children settled themselves in, 'borrowing' my spare

Christmas cards and stamps, Sellotape and wrapping paper
– just as they did every year – and squabbling over the
ribbon and tags. All of that, plus the ironing board being set
up in the sitting room, and the smell of everyone's favourite
meal cooking, finally made my new house feel like a real
home at last.

We were still a family, and if only Alice could bring herself
to accept our changed circumstances I was sure she would
soon realize that. Knowing Alice as I did, I realized that was
going to take time.

Perhaps I should have waited longer to start dating, but
when would the right time be? I had hardly ordered Stuart
to ask me out, in fact no one was more surprised than me
when he did – or more surprised than me when I accepted.
At least it gave a clear message that I was moving on with
my life and it would appear that only Alice, of the five children, was the one to have a problem with that.

Even Owen had seemed to accept it after his first few
strops, and maybe it would help if he followed my example
and found a lady of his own. I was rather taken by surprise
at just how odd the thought of seeing him with someone else
made me feel. A definite case of dog in the manger attitude,
I realized and I began to sympathize, rather belatedly, with
his strange behaviour – though I had no intention of
emulating it when the time came. I would make absolutely
certain that I was one of the very first to wish him happy.

We had both accepted years ago that we would never be
together as a regular couple, but had obviously become very
used to the arrangement that meant we had all the perks of
a relationship, but none of the aggravation that arose when

sex became part of the equation. There was a lot to be said for platonic liaisons – as ours had proved to us both time and again over the years.

'You've gone quiet,' Mai commented from where she was wrestling paper round an oddly shaped parcel, 'and you've ironed that blouse sleeve three times now.'

I looked up, my thoughts still miles away. 'Oh, have I?'

'Yes,' Ella agreed, looking up from setting the table. 'If you're trying to get into Alice's mind and work out what she will do next, I strongly recommend you give up now, because I doubt even she knows.'

'True.' Connor joined in, coming through the door with a pile of neatly wrapped packages in his arms and kneeling down to add them to the growing heap under the tree. 'You've always told us not to worry about something you can't do anything about – and you can't do anything about Alice or her refusal to accept that you are entitled to a life of your own. She'll let you know soon enough what her next move is going to be.' He turned out to be absolutely right.

It was early evening and thankfully we had already enjoyed most of our meal and were sitting chatting comfortably for a while to allow the main course time to go down before starting on the pudding. Arthur was telling us that it was a very long while since he'd shared a family meal and he had then gone on to say how much he was looking forward to Christmas this year, when the doorbell went.

My heart lurched as Gizmo ran barking along the hall, and I was really fervently hoping that Stuart hadn't taken it upon himself to turn up unannounced after we had agreed that any meetings we found time for should be away from the house until after Christmas. Before anyone could move the doorbell pealed again, and we all went to move at once, except Arthur.

'I'll go.' Connor waved his hands at the rest of us. 'It'll probably be carol singers.'

'There's some pound coins in the dish on the hall table,' I called after him.

The sound of a kerfuffle could clearly be heard. Connor's reasonable tone kept low, then the door flew open and Alice stood there. She had obviously spent the day winding herself up and she looked furious, but also very beautiful with her long blonde hair tumbling in messy curls past her shoulders. However angry she undoubtedly was, Alice, being Alice, had still taken the time to apply her usual immaculate make-up and to choose her clothes with care.

All of this flitted through my mind in the short silence as we stared at her and she stared back at us.

'Sorry,' Connor said from behind her. 'I did try to stop her.'

'There was no need, Connor.' I produced a welcoming smile from somewhere. 'Alice knows she's always welcome here – just as you all are. Come on in and join us, Alice. We were about to enjoy Ella's apple pie – your favourite.' I went towards her. 'Let me take your coat and then come and meet Arthur.'

She shrugged my hands away from her long black wool coat.

'Don't touch me.' She stared, long and hard, at the remains of the meal on the table, at the two girls and Arthur still sitting at the table, and her blue eyes glittered. Her tone was at first sarcastic. 'How *very* cosy,' and then disbelieving as she gave Arthur her full attention, 'and please don't tell me *that's* the new boyfriend.'

Arthur smiled at her, seeming quite unfazed. 'I wish I could say I had that honour.' He stood up and held out his hand. 'I'm Evie's next door neighbour.'

Alice dismissed him rudely, ignoring his words and his outstretched hand to address me. 'So,' she said bitterly, 'everyone is welcome in your precious new home except Owen, and after all he did for us – after all he did for you.'

I felt as if she had slapped me and then heard Owen himself speak from behind her, his voice ringing out as he snapped, 'That's quite enough, Alice.'

She turned, and looked chastened, but only for the briefest moment; she turned her attention back to me as if he had never spoken. 'How *could* you?' she hissed, 'What kind of mother are you to tear this family apart?'

This was too much for me and I had to fight to keep calm. 'Does this family really look to you as if it's been torn apart?' I indicated my younger daughter and Owen's, still sitting next to each other at the table with Arthur, also Connor, Owen and now Jake standing in the doorway. 'Nothing has changed, Alice, except that we *all* now live at different addresses – even *you* do.'

'*You* were the first to leave,' Connor pointed out in what he obviously thought was a reasonable tone.

'Oh.' She turned on him furiously. 'I might have known I would get the blame.'

'That's not what he meant, Alice.' Jake came into the room and put an arm around Alice's shoulders. I noticed that she didn't shake him off as she had me.

'Look, why don't you come and join us?' I pleaded, eager to calm the situation down. 'All of you. We can enjoy Ella's pie and talk about this calmly and rationally.'

'That sounds like a good idea, doesn't it?' Jake tried to draw Alice to the table and Mai pulled a chair out for her sister.

'Not to me it doesn't and I can't believe you think so. She's ruined everything and now she wants us to sit down together and pretend it's all fine. Well, I won't do it.' Alice tore herself away from Jake, pushing both Connor and Owen aside, as she made for the door.

'What exactly *is* your problem, Alice?' I asked, making sure that my voice rose clearly above the hubbub as everyone seemed to speak at once. 'What have I done that's so very wrong?'

She paused and then said with a scowl, 'You know.'

'Actually, I don't.'

'You split the family up.'

'The family hasn't split up.' Owen pointed this out, which saved me from doing so. 'We're all here, together, just as we always will be for all the special occasions. We'll be together on Christmas Day, just like most families with grown-up children, before we all go back to our own lives and own homes.'

'So she gets to host Christmas and play happy families for one day because it suits her. Well, I won't do it.'

I suddenly felt unutterably weary. 'Do you know what, Alice?' She glared at me, and suddenly I had had enough. I said, 'That's your choice and the last thing I would want to do is to try and force you to join us. You have your invitation: whether or not you choose to accept it is entirely up to you.'

There was complete silence, then Alice spun on her high-heeled boots. There was an almighty crash as the front door was slammed – so hard that the sound seemed to reverberate for quite some time – behind her.

Eleven

That was that, then. I had called Alice's bluff and now, for the first time in fifteen years, the family wouldn't all be together on Christmas Day. The very thought broke my heart. There was only one thing left to do and I did it. Bursting into tears was an absolute relief.

'She doesn't mean it,' Jake said, though he didn't sound too sure to me. 'I'll go after her.'

The two girls rushed to comfort me, poor Arthur sat there looking totally confused, but Owen suddenly and unexpectedly applauded. We all stared at him.

Then Connor laughed and also clapped his hands. 'Bravo, Mum. It's about time someone stood up to her. There are five of us – and Owen – and it's not all about Alice. God knows what her problem is, I'm not even sure *she* knows.'

'Even though life changes for all of us all the time she seems to think that whatever suits her can simply remain the same,' Ella commented sourly. 'Like a huge family house being kept just for special occasions like Christmas, with

Dad and Evie living together in it regardless of any wishes they might have. Doesn't she realize that, even if they *were* in the relationship she so clearly wants them to be in, they would probably have downsized anyway, once we all left home?'

'Do you mind if I say something?' Arthur asked quietly.

'Oh, Arthur,' I clapped my hand to my mouth, 'I'm so sorry. We invite you to join us for a meal and then you have to sit and listen to a huge family argument.'

He smiled his calm smile, seeming quite unperturbed. 'All families have arguments,' he pointed out, 'and mine was no different. She's scared, your Alice, that's all.'

'Alice – scared?'

I could tell it was all that Connor could do not to openly scoff at what he saw as a ridiculous statement and, even while I frowned a warning at him, I couldn't help thinking he had a point. Alice had always given the impression that she was afraid of nothing and nobody and I had absolutely no reason to doubt that.

'Scared of what?' Mai asked, staring at Arthur.

'Is she the eldest in the family?' he asked.

'Well, no.' I was the one who replied. 'Jake – the lad who went after her – is older by a year.'

Arthur nodded. 'And she was how old when her father left?'

Owen provided the information and I could tell he was taken with what Arthur was saying. 'She was seven, Jake eight, and the younger ones were three, four and five respectively.'

'Old enough to recall the fear and uncertainty she felt at

that time; rejected too, I wouldn't doubt, and to be afraid of feeling like that again – even at her age.'

'But Jake...' Connor began.

'... was older and I understand that. Probably – like the younger ones – he was able to accept the changes more easily and, to be blunt,' Arthur pointed out, 'although it was terrible that his mother died, she didn't *choose* to leave him, did she?'

Mai nodded her head. 'Yes,' she said, 'there is a difference. I just chose not to dwell on it. I suppose that was easy for me because I barely remember my biological father and Owen filled that position so beautifully that I can't say I ever missed him.'

'Me, too,' Connor agreed.

Owen looked as if he might be the next one to burst into tears as he said gruffly, 'Thanks, guys. That's wonderful to hear and it means the world to me.'

'So,' I looked to Arthur for guidance, 'what do you think we should do about Alice?'

'I don't think you have to do anything very much at all, Evie, except to let her know that you love her and the door is always open. In her heart she does already know that, of course, and I don't doubt she will come round in her own good time.'

'How come you're so wise?' Ella went and sat next to Arthur and gazed at him adoringly; Mai quickly sat in the chair on his other side.

'If I am,' he chuckled, 'it's because I've seen a little bit more of life at my age and have hopefully learned from what I've seen.'

'Sit down, everyone,' I called over my shoulder as I made my way into the kitchen. 'We can't let Ella's apple pie go to waste. Yes, you, too, Owen, there's plenty to go round.'

'So that's what happened.' I finished telling Stuart the whole story when we met up the night before Christmas Eve.

A quick drink at the local pub was all we had time for, what with my last-minute preparations and a job he was determined would be completed before the festive holiday officially commenced. He had been late arriving and I thought he looked tired.

'At least they all know I exist now.'

He seemed pleased about that and I felt obliged to point out, 'Yes, but that wasn't at all the right way for them to be told that I was seeing someone, Stuart, and Sandy had absolutely no right to take it upon herself. She's not even family. I told you I would do it when we had everyone together, and I would have.'

'Dropping that into the conversation might have ruined your family celebrations on Christmas Day,' Stuart pointed out.

'Well,' I reminded him, 'it's done that anyway. I'm sure that Alice will be conspicuous by her absence, and probably Jake as well.'

'In that case,' Stuart said, making what seemed to me to be an obvious effort not to appear too eager, 'I might just as well come and join you for lunch – now that everyone knows about me.'

'I thought you'd planned to spend the day with your parents.' I tried not to show how much I disliked the idea of him hijacking a family Christmas that I felt needed careful handling.

'Plans are made to be changed.'

'Not mine – and especially not this year,' I found myself saying firmly. 'Mine were – and are – for one last family Christmas. You can come and meet everyone once the festivities are over and, if we're still together next year, I can promise you that things will be very different and you'll be more than welcome to join us.'

'Thank you.'

I thought there was a hint of sarcasm in Stuart's tone but, as I reminded myself, he was just one person and a very new addition to my life; for this year at least I had already decided that my family had to come first. I had a feeling that if he turned up to lunch, even if Alice didn't, it would be the final straw for her when she heard about it. I wasn't willing to take that chance.

Thankfully, the subject was dropped and we both made a determined effort to make the most of the brief time we could spend together. Stuart had come straight from work and I loved the way he looked a little rough around the edges, his curly hair over-long and unruly, the stubble on his chin grown into more of a beard.

'Sorry I don't look my usual well-turned-out self,' he said at one point, smoothing his checked shirt self-consciously. 'If I'd gone home to shower and change first we'd have had no time at all.'

'Actually, Stuart,' I was smiling as I leaned forward and looked deeply into his dark eyes, 'you don't have to apologize. I quite kind of like being out with a bit of rough for a change.'

'*Do* you?' He held my gaze with his and I could feel myself growing hotter at my awareness of the clear desire he made no attempt to hide. 'Keep looking at me like that and I shall be climbing right across this table or,' he growled deeply, 'we could go back to my place right now and you could share the shower with me.'

It had been so long since anybody had so blatantly wanted me, even longer since I had wanted to throw caution to the wind and snatch what was clearly on offer and worry about the consequences later. It was Stuart who put the brakes on and I honestly didn't know whether to be glad or really very sorry when I thought about it later.

'Only joking,' he said with a wry smile. 'It wouldn't be very special if you had to climb out of my bed in the early hours and go home to face a barrage of questions – and I do want the first time to be special for both of us. I know that's what you want too.'

'Mmm,' I agreed and wondered if he realized how very close I had been to snatching up my coat, grabbing his hand, and simply living in the moment.

Perhaps he did, because though he kissed me until my head was spinning, before we parted to go our separate ways he was the one to break away and hold me at arm's length to say, 'Good night, Evie.' I really appreciated the fact that he added, 'Have a lovely Christmas Day with your family – and I hope that Alice comes round.'

'Thank you for being so understanding and have a good day with your parents.'

'See you on Boxing Day,' he called through the open window of his van, 'and we can make up for lost time.'

I didn't think anyone could grudge me that, I mused on the way home, but I knew without a doubt that Alice would.

They were all spending that day with Owen. She would be furious that I wasn't there – even if she intended to spend the day ignoring me for daring to have a life – and a man – of my own.

Christmas Eve day the house became a hive of activity, as everyone rushed around polishing and cleaning, and rushing out to the shops for last-minute purchases. It was only when someone asked, out of the blue, if I was making my own stuffing that I remembered the fresh turkey had yet to be collected from the local butcher's. Connor volunteered to help me manhandle it home.

'Can you imagine Christmas Day with no turkey?' I was laughing as we made our way home, but inside I was only just getting over the feeling of panic when I had discovered my oversight, though the butcher had assured me he would have phoned, or even delivered it in person.

'I'm sure you have a chicken or two in the freezer,' Connor said with a smile, easy-going as ever. 'How big is this beast, anyway? You're still going to be eating it curried long after we've all gone back to our various universities and jobs.'

I was just explaining that Owen would have that privilege, because all the left-over cold meat was destined to find its way to his house to form the basis for his Boxing Day buffet, when the elderly lady a couple of doors down stopped at her gate and said, 'See you later. What time would you like us to come round?'

I simply stared at her, because I was recalling with absolute clarity that she'd said quite definitely that they wouldn't be accepting my invitation. When Connor nudged me with the turkey I realized that my mouth was hanging open. I closed it with a snap and recovered enough to say in a strangled tone, 'Erm, any time after seven will be fine.'

'Look forward to seeing you,' Connor said cheerfully, then, addressing me out of the corner of his mouth, he muttered, 'You didn't say we were having a party.'

'It was just meant to be drinks, and those who didn't refuse the invitation point blank – like the lady who just spoke to us – didn't bother to reply. What on earth am I going to do if they all turn up?' The panic I'd experienced over the forgotten turkey had returned with a vengeance and I could hear it in my voice.

'I can't believe you're worrying about having a few neighbours over for nibbles, Mum, when you used to feed an army of hungry kids at a moment's notice?' Connor said from behind me while I fumbled to get the key in the door, suddenly a complete bag of nerves. 'Our friends were always dropping round uninvited and you'd rustle up a feast in no time. At least you've had a bit of warning.'

'Had a warning about what?' Mai demanded. 'Don't tell me that Alice is on her way over?'

'No, just that a few neighbours are popping round tonight. Mum's getting in a right tizz about it,' he dismissed easily.

'A party?' Ella beamed. 'Oh, I love a party. We'll help you, won't we, Mai?'

At least, I thought, surveying our efforts later – some of which I would admit only to my nearest and dearest being the result of a quick trip to M & S and Iceland just before they closed – we had come up with a reasonable spread between us.

We were standing around, dressed in our posh frocks and

sipping drinks while we waited to see if some – or indeed any – of the neighbours were going to turn up, when the doorbell rang.

Connor, who had probably taken the longest to get ready and whose efforts would just about run to a clean T-shirt and jeans and freshly gelled hair, could be heard clattering down the stairs. 'I'll get it,' he called.

I said comfortably, 'That will be Arthur. At least we can count on him not to let us down.'

It *was* Arthur, but he wasn't alone because a couple of neighbours I scarcely recognized followed him through and from then on there was a steady procession. Soon my kitchen and dining room-cum-sitting room was quite crowded.

'I know I said we wouldn't come,' the elderly lady confided, 'but then I thought how unsociable we were being. It is Christmas, after all.'

'People don't mix any more, eh'm afraid,' said my immediate neighbour on the opposite side from Arthur, 'and we're the worst culprits, aren't we, Giles?'

'Indeed,' he agreed, appearing to savour red wine swept hastily from the bargain bin at the off-licence an hour or so earlier. 'Problem is that commuting takes up far too much time.'

The elderly contingency were soon comfortably ensconced on the couches at the sitting room end of the room with Arthur in the centre encouraging a lively discussion, while everyone else milled around chatting, eating and drinking at the other end.

I was amazed, first that anyone had bothered to turn up after the very unpromising response to my invitations, and secondly by how well everyone was getting on. I felt I could relax and enjoy myself, and recognized that a huge part of the success of the evening was down to the children and their help with the last-minute preparation.

I watched proudly as Mai circulated with plates of nibbles and Connor followed with a bottle in each hand offering top-ups. Ella was sitting with Arthur and chatting as animatedly to the pensioners as if she were with a bunch of her own friends.

Watching them, I thought what a great job Owen and I had done of bringing up our two families together; I wished he was there to share the moment of pleasure and pride in our achievement. I suddenly really missed his tall, reassuring presence by my side and was surprised to feel a real stab of regret that this year, for the first time in fifteen years, we would be waking up in different houses on Christmas Day.

Twelve

'Well, that was a bit mad, wasn't it?' Connor commented when the last of my neighbours had, with a great show of believable reluctance, headed for home. The unlikely promises that it would be their turn next time still rang in our ears.

'Mad is the word,' I agreed, shaking my head in disbelief. 'I'm not sure how I ended up with a houseful like that when those I actually spoke to refused my invitation quite emphatically and the rest didn't even bother to reply. I wonder what changed their minds?'

We surveyed the empty wine glasses on every available surface and the piles of dirty plates, also empty, and automatically all made a move to make a start on the clearing-up. Despite the lateness of the hour we knew without saying a word that this was one time when the mess couldn't possibly be left until tomorrow.

'Just goes to show it only takes one person making an effort for things to start changing.' Ella looked up from loading the dishwasher.

'Yeah,' Mai nodded, 'and who knows, your little get-together tonight might just be the start of a nice friendly close-knit community. They seemed very nice people, just a bit too wrapped up in their own lives. Well done, Mum.'

With the four of us mucking in the work was soon done, and I had the turkey stuffed, draped with streaky bacon slices, and in the oven on a low heat before I eventually took myself off to bed, still basking in the children's warm approval.

Owen was on the doorstep practically at first light and, as I let him in, I glanced hopefully over his shoulder. The driveway behind him remained stubbornly empty apart from the cars, and I felt my hopes and my heart plummet with disappointment when it was clear that he had come alone.

'Merry Christmas,' I said, kissing a cheek that had obviously been freshly shaved and smelled of a very pleasant cologne. 'You're bright and early, though not nearly early enough to catch the girls still slumbering. They've been up since five o'clock and have been feeling their way through the packages and guessing at the contents while they were waiting for everyone else to be here.'

It was tradition that no one opened a present until we were all together on Christmas morning and, even as very small children, they had adhered to this unspoken rule. I wondered what would happen when it dawned on them that this year it would be different.

Hearing his voice the girls rushed into the hall to hug Owen, throwing their arms around his neck, but I didn't miss the hopeful peeps towards the door, or the disappointment on both their faces when they realized, as I had, that he had come alone.

Another tradition was the full English breakfast that had always been served on Christmas morning. Ridiculous when you considered the huge lunch that would be following in a relatively short time, but there had been a hue and cry whenever Owen or I tried to suggest that toast and cereal would be a lot easier and far less filling.

I went to make a start. Before I had turned the grilling bacon and sausages even once, Connor came in, sniffing appreciatively. I could tell that at a glance he had taken in the fact we were short on numbers, and held my breath, knowing that Connor of all people could be counted upon to say what everyone else was thinking.

We probably all exhaled when he merely took his seat at the table and said cheerfully, 'If any extra bacon going could find its way onto my plate you'll find it won't go to waste.'

He set the pattern. The atmosphere lightened considerably and became determinedly cheerful from then on, but there was no denying that there was an elephant in the room that was hard to ignore as we tucked into the traditional breakfast and then ooh-ed and ah-ed over our gifts.

This was the first year Owen and I hadn't pooled our resources for the bigger presents but, in spite of this, the children had done very well out of us. Mindful of their student status our gifts consisted of up-dated mobile phones, iTunes vouchers and every other kind of voucher, mainly for preferred high-street stores, together with useful things like socks, underwear and warm dressing gowns.

I had bought Owen jokey gifts, just as I always had done,

because it didn't feel right not to. This year he received a doorbell offering a range of tunes from God Save the Queen to the William Tell overture (because his house only had a knocker), a kitchen timer and half a dozen eggs (because it was well-known that he couldn't boil an egg, though he was a good cook in most other areas) and a subscription to a popular women's magazine (because it was an open secret that he'd enjoyed reading any copies of mine left lying around and the girls' periodicals when he thought we weren't looking).

My main present was return flights to Scotland and hotel accommodation for a brief stay in the area where he grew up. Owen had been born in the Highlands to parents already in their forties and, though he had lived in England since he was quite a young man and had all but lost his accent, he still described himself to anyone who would listen as a Scotsman. He had never returned since his parents had died some years before, but was forever saying that he intended to.

I enjoyed his evident pleasure in the gift, and managed to dismiss the thought of the often repeated promise that he would take me there and show me his boyhood haunts by reminding myself quite firmly that times had changed.

The majority of the gifts I received consisted of pretty earrings, which were my weakness, perfume, and lots of stationery items for my office. There was an uncomfortable moment when it became apparent that my main gift, a joint one from them all, it would appear, was currently in the possession of the two absentees.

There was a huge effort made by those who *were* present

not to show how annoyed they were, and by me to show even more pleasure over the thoughtful presents I had already received. We all tried not to notice the sad little heap of wrapped and labelled presents still sitting waiting to be claimed under the Christmas tree.

The girls and I busied ourselves in the kitchen, clearing all signs of breakfast and making sure that lunch preparations were going according to plan and nothing had been forgotten. Owen and Connor were left to collect up discarded wrapping paper and deposit piles of gifts on the recipients' beds or in corners out of the way.

'Can one of you please check on Arthur and arrange to collect him before lunch?' I looked up from arranging cocktail sausages wrapped in bacon in regimental lines on a baking tray. 'He's looking forward to raising a glass of sherry with us.'

'I'll go,' Owen said immediately. 'It was really quite icy out there first thing – I wouldn't be surprised to see a flurry of snow – and we wouldn't want him to slip.' With that he was gone.

'Sherry?' Connor was staring at me as if I was mad. 'Since when did we ever drink sherry?'

'I don't think I've ever tasted it,' Ella said, and Mai added, 'me either. Why are we having it today?'

'I know we never drank sherry before,' I agreed, and went on to say firmly, 'but we will be raising a glass each today, because it used to be a tradition for Arthur and his late wife, Rose, to enjoy a toast before their Christmas lunch. He still does it every year, but he hasn't had anyone to raise a glass with – until now.'

'Oh, well, sherry all round it is then,' Connor said without hesitation and offered, 'I can set the glasses out – tumblers or wine glasses?'

'A tumbler full of sherry would see us all under the table,' I said laughing. 'If I remember correctly, my parents had some very small wine glasses they used and I think you'll find some that will suit in that cupboard there. I probably won them in a raffle or something. I don't think they've ever been used because sherry isn't my tipple either – but for Arthur....'

'For Arthur we'll drink sherry and we'll enjoy it.' Mai smiled. 'Is he bringing Gizmo?'

'We couldn't leave him out on Christmas Day, could we?' Ella grinned, 'and anyway, I've brought him a present.'

'Me, too,' Mai said.

Connor looked dismayed. 'Well, I wish you'd said before, because I didn't even think of it.'

'Chop him up some turkey finely at lunchtime and he'll be perfectly happy, I assure you,' I soothed, then realized that the very dog was making his way into the room followed by Owen on the other end of his lead.

'Where's Arthur?' we all asked when it became clear that he wasn't following.

'He's coming a bit later,' Owen explained, 'after he's Skyped his family, but I've said I'll walk Gizmo for him because it's very cold and those pavements are quite slippery.'

'I'll come.'

'And me.'

'Me, too.'

In no time at all I found myself alone in the house. The sudden silence was deafening and I found myself reaching to turn the radio on, thinking it funny how quickly I had become used to having the sounds of family around me again.

Everything I could do had eventually been done, the various items that made up Christmas lunch were either roasting, steaming or simmering and the walkers still weren't back, so I settled down with a cup of coffee.

Carols were playing softly on the radio, the lights were twinkling on the tree, the smell of good food filled the air and we would soon be seated around the table to enjoy it. I smiled and thought that it was very nearly perfect, despite the upheaval of the past few months it felt as if we had survived as a family – almost.

The sound of the doorbell was a relief, banishing as it did thoughts of Alice, who would allow her own chagrin with me, to keep her away from the rest of her family on such a special day.

'I thought you were never coming back,' I was saying cheerfully, as I swung the door back to reveal Alice and Jake on the step.

'Well, we weren't if I'd had my way,' she said flatly, stepping past me. Jake, following, managed an apologetic expression and a quick shrug as he walked by.

Alice drew up short when a swift glance told her that no one else was in the house and Jake cannoned straight into her. 'Where is everyone?' she demanded.

'At the park down the road, I presume, with Gizmo – Arthur's dog,' I explained, adding, 'I thought you were them coming back. You're very welcome.'

I followed them into the big room, suddenly very conscious that the table had been set for only six, and that it would be quite clear we hadn't been expecting them.

'We thought we should be here today, didn't we, Alice?' Jake encouraged, though it was quite obvious it was he, and not Alice, who'd had the thought.

'I'm here for the sake of the others – not you,' she said rudely to me, prompting Jake to protest, 'Alice!'

'Well, it's true, and I'm not going to pretend otherwise, but if we're not welcome....' She had obviously spotted the table arrangements and taken umbrage, even though it was clear that if she'd had her way she would be elsewhere.

'You must know that you are *all* welcome in my home, any time,' I said quietly.

'Oh, yes,' her voice was loaded with sarcasm, 'I know that just about *everyone* is welcome in *your* home.'

Her nasty tone prompted me to protest. 'I really don't know what your problem is, Alice. I am a grown-up single woman; am I not allowed a man friend, because I guess that's what you are referring to?'

'Perhaps it was the fact that you couldn't wait for us to be gone before you embarked on this affair,' she glared at me, 'and the fact that you were so secretive about it. As if,' she snarled, 'you had something to hide.'

I was about to protest, to reiterate what I had said before about waiting until they were all together, when Jake – who had been staring at her in the strangest way – suddenly spoke.

'Sometimes,' he said, 'I feel as if I don't even know you, Alice, because how you can say that, you of all people—'

She seemed to know what he was going to say and she hastened to interrupt him. 'This has nothing to do with that. It's entirely different.'

'How?' he demanded. 'How is it different?'

Ever the peacemaker, Jake gave in to Alice's whims and humours more than anyone else in the family. It was why they got on so well, and because I had never known Jake to challenge Alice before, I found myself staring at him.

'It just is,' she said sullenly, throwing Jake a look that would normally have shut him up.

Today it didn't seem to be working, because he was insisting on an answer, demanding, 'How exactly, Alice?' then continuing astonishingly: 'you can't answer, can you, Alice? Your mum has asked you more than once what your problem is and I would like to know the answer to that question. Why is it so wrong for your mum to have a secret boyfriend, but it's all right that you do?'

I looked from one to the other and shook my head. 'Well, I can see why Alice might think I was trying to keep Stuart a secret, but I thought I'd explained that I was simply waiting to tell you I was seeing someone when you were all together. It's not even anything serious because we haven't been seeing each other for long.'

'Oh.' Jake smiled, but it wasn't a pleasant smile. 'Alice can't say it isn't serious because she's been seeing her secret boyfriend for some time. Haven't you, Alice?'

'Shut up, Jake,' she said, but it came out as more of a plea than the order she would usually have issued.

'I won't shut up because this has been going on for long enough and I'd like to know how you can accuse your mum of being secretive when you're guilty of the same thing your-self.' Jake sounded incensed and as if he had been holding his anger in for a very long time. 'You're a hypocrite, Alice, and have made me into one, too.'

I felt I had to step in and cool the situation down before it got out of hand. I wasn't sure what was going on here, but I tried to make light of it by saying, 'I'm sure Alice doesn't have to tell me – us – every detail of her life, including whoever she is seeing. She's an adult now and may do as she pleases, see whom she pleases.'

'She doesn't afford you the same privilege though, does she?' he pointed out.

There was nothing I could say to that, so instead I said, 'Perhaps Alice thinks we will disapprove.'

'We both do,' Jake said bluntly, 'because her secret boyfriend is me.'

There was a sudden audible intake of breath from the doorway, and the three of us turned to find Owen, Connor, Ella and Mai standing in the doorway. It was obvious that they had heard every word.

Thirteen

Alice stood white-faced, all trace of defiance had been wiped from her expression and Jake stood close beside her. He appeared to be rigid with the magnitude of his announcement and was obviously waiting for something – wrath, disapproval, disappointment, disgust – anything from the family to fall around their ears.

In all honesty we were probably so shocked, stunned even, by such a startling revelation that I don't think any of us could think of a single thing to say. To be told that Alice and Jake were a couple, out of the blue like that – and had been for some time, it would appear – was something none of us had been expecting, judging by the stunned looks on everybody's faces.

None of us knew how to react, though it must have been obvious to everyone that something was going to have to be said but, for the moment at least, all we could manage was an astounded silence. Into the silence Noddy Holder of the seventies band Slade suddenly yelled, 'It's Christmas!' from the radio that must have been playing quietly and unnoticed, and it was just what I needed to prompt me into action as the popular festive song continued on the radio.

I carefully kept my tone even as I said, 'I'm sure we all have something to say, but before anybody says anything in haste that they might come to regret, I think we should sit down and enjoy the lunch we've spent all morning preparing. It's Christmas and we're all together as a family; any discussion can wait until later, can't it?'

'Of course it can.' Owen instantly followed my lead and I was so grateful to him. 'I'll go and get Arthur.' He left immediately and I had the feeling he couldn't get out of the door quickly enough. I didn't blame him one bit, because if I felt completely out of my depth there was no doubt at all that he felt the same.

'I'll set two more places.' Ella rushed to busy herself rearranging the table settings.

'I'll help dish up, Mum.' Mai followed me into the kitchen area. I had the feeling she was wishing she could shut a door behind her but it was probably just as well that that wasn't possible in an open plan house like this one. It wouldn't help at all, I felt sure, for anyone to be suspected of whispering in corners.

'You could open your presents,' Connor offered helpfully, indicating the untouched pile under the tree.

'Perhaps later,' Jake managed, with a quick look at Alice, who hadn't moved since he had dropped his bombshell into our midst.

Gizmo proved a welcome distraction, racing around the room and tearing up to each person in turn, delighted to find even more new people. Even Alice, it seemed, couldn't resist his overtures and she sank on to a chair, lifting him into her arms and allowing him to lick a cheek that was as pale as alabaster.

In the end I couldn't have been more amazed or pleased at how well lunch went. In spite of what had just happened, everyone made a concerted effort to behave normally. Arthur was, of course, completely unaware of any slight atmosphere and he positively beamed as we each raised a glass of sherry in Rose's memory. Then he encouraged us to toast each other's health, and to empty our glasses – which we did for his sake with every appearance of enjoyment.

It probably really helped what could have been a difficult situation to have Arthur there, because he was so obviously thoroughly enjoying the food and the company that we all went out of our way to ensure nothing happened to spoil it for him.

Crackers were pulled, paper hats were worn by everyone, and mottos read and embellished with our own touches of humour. The impression that this was exactly the same as any other Christmas lunch we had shared was somehow achieved, and most of us ate with a good appetite. In fact, I found I was actually starving, but then it was a well-known fact that I was inclined to eat more in times of stress.

Jake and Alice had been separated at the table, but whether this had been by accident or design on Ella's part when she had directed everyone to their places, I had no way of knowing. He continually sent worried glances Alice's way, but Arthur seemed to be doing an excellent job of drawing her out and, in the end she was chatting to him quite amicably and I even heard her laugh once or twice.

At last, when the pudding had been set on fire as tradition dictated, and then eaten with either ice cream, custard, cream or brandy butter – or even, as in a couple of cases, a mixture of several of these choices – Arthur excused himself because Rose's sister had promised to ring him. Connor, Ella and Mai immediately insisted that they would see him home safely and begged to be allowed to take Gizmo for another walk while he was waiting for his call.

That left Owen and me with Jake and Alice and a silence we didn't quite know how to even begin to fill. It took all my willpower not to start rushing around clearing up the debris of the meal we had just eaten, but somehow I managed it.

It was, typically, Alice who eventually broke the silence with a brave show of her usual defiance. 'You'd just as well give us *all* the reasons you can come up with why Jake and I shouldn't be together, because I'm sure they are many and varied.' She glared at Owen and me. 'It's what we've been expecting and why we've kept quiet. We probably know them all, but we can't help the way we feel.'

'What are they?' I asked calmly.

'What?' Alice stared at me, obviously taken aback.

'The reasons why you shouldn't be together: what are they?'

'You know.'

'Well, actually I don't.' I shrugged, and turning to Owen asked him. 'Do you?'

He frowned, 'Well, I could probably guess at a couple, but I'm not sure if they'd be valid or not. Our circumstances are – unusual.'

'Oh.' Alice actually seemed lost for words, then she

managed to demand, 'So why the big show of disapproval from everyone when Jake made his announcement?'

'I think you'll find it was more surprise than disapproval,' I ventured, and Owen nodded in agreement. 'It wasn't something we were expecting to hear, that's all.'

'But we're stepbrother and stepsister,' Jake pointed out in a troubled tone.

'Actually, you aren't,' Owen rebutted, 'because Evie and I aren't married or even in a relationship. We shared a house because that's the way we decided to do things, but we could almost as easily have been living next door to one another. The relationships would still have been similar. If you're worried about the family connection we can soon check out the legalities of the matter, though you aren't related in any way.'

'You may have grown up together,' I added, 'but you two were seven and eight years old when we all got together, not babies, and you knew from the start that we were two families, not one. We did our best to make that clear to you all and that knowledge has probably made a difference to your feelings now.'

'Why are you being so understanding?' Alice demanded suddenly, looking straight at me.

'You're my daughter, why wouldn't I be?' I asked, returning her look with a straight one of my own.

'Because I've behaved like such a bitch to you recently.'

'It's not been easy these last months for any of us.'

'But I've punished you and blamed you for daring to want a life of your own – and all the time I knew deep in my heart that I had no right to object.' Tears trickled down her face and all the defiance and anger seemed to have left her as she continued, 'you and Owen couldn't have been straighter with us if you tried.

'Right from the start we were all well aware that our family and your relationship wasn't what it seemed, we had to tell people often enough, but there's never been a day go by when I didn't want for us to be *exactly* what we seemed. I know it's childish, but I never once gave up hope – until everything changed and forced me to accept that to keep hoping was pointless. Then I just got angry – with you. I guess I just needed someone to blame for making changes I wasn't ready for.'

'Oh, Alice,' I said.

She shrugged. 'That seems a bit ridiculous in the light of what you now know about Jake and me, but I wanted everything at home to stay the same forever and was furious that you didn't want the same. You and Owen did such a great job, healing us from all the hurt the five of us had been through. You were always such great parents and I loved the security of you being together so much that I suppose your relationship became real to me.

She smiled ruefully and continued, 'I can't believe I've been so selfish, only thinking about what I wanted. I even managed to convince myself that you would marry each other one day and Owen would become my dad in reality. It's only now I can finally see that it really doesn't matter at all that I call you Owen.' She turned to him and said, with the sweetest smile, 'because you're my dad in every single way that counts – the best dad in the world.'

Owen looked as if he might cry himself as he told her,

'Thank you. It means the world to me to hear you say that. I hope you realize now, Alice, that though circumstances may change, feelings don't. When we all moved in together I became the father of five children and that will never change. The fact that your mum and I live in different houses now won't ever mean I love you any less. You're a social worker and should know, of all people, that similar things happen even in traditional families.'

'I know,' she hung her head, 'but knowing the theory doesn't help very much when it happens to you. Thank you, both of you, for being so reasonable and accepting. I have a feeling I've learned a lot about myself and about life in general and maybe I can be a more understanding social worker as a result.'

We smiled at each other, but there was no time to say more as the dog-walkers erupted into the room, minus Gizmo who, they explained was back with Arthur.

'He's having a bit of a rest,' Connor explained, 'and I've told him not, under any circumstances, to make the attempt to come round here on his own because one of us will go and collect him later and ensure he arrives safely. The temperature is already dropping out there and Arthur reckons snow is forecast.'

'Shall we start clearing up?' Mai started collecting pudding dishes, but I stopped her and invited, 'Sit down for a bit – all of you. We can do it later. Jake was about to tell us how he and Alice got together and what their plans for the future are.'

Jake actually looked a bit startled, which was hardly surprising since he had indicated no such thing and, in fact, had said hardly a word since making his defiant announcement.

'Yes, go on, Jake,' Alice encouraged as the other three sat down and looked at the pair of them expectantly.

'Well,' he started hesitantly, 'we haven't been together very long at all in spite of what I said, or really made any plans either. It was all the upheaval; you know, everyone going their separate ways and then the family house being sold. It felt like the last straw to Alice. She was absolutely devastated.'

Reaching over he took her hand in his, looking at her in such a caring way that I felt tears pricking my eyelids. 'She knew she was overreacting, didn't you?'

Alice nodded, pulled a rueful face and shrugged an apology to the rest of us.

'She couldn't help how she felt, but that was when she turned to me. She knew I would understand how she felt.'

I had a sudden vision of them coming together to the restaurant to find Owen and me on the day that Mai went off to university, and the For Sale board went up on the house.

He paused, and then went on, 'I was just a shoulder to cry on at first – and I knew that – but you see, I've been in love with Alice for a very long time – and these past weeks she's come to share my feelings.'

'Oh, Jake – Alice,' Mai was crying, 'that's so sweet.'

'It's all right for them to be together, isn't it?' Connor looked from Owen to me.

'We have no objection,' Owen said emphatically, 'and as they are not related in any way I don't think there can be any legal problem, but that's something that can be easily clarified. If necessary we can speak to a solicitor.'

'Well, I think it's lovely,' Ella said. 'Who would have thought it?' She frowned suddenly and warned, 'Just don't start expecting me to fancy Connor because it's just not going to happen.'

At the look of complete horror on both their faces the rest of us burst out laughing and they very quickly joined in.

'Let's hurry up now and get the lunch things cleared away,' I said, still smiling, 'and then we can get Arthur round to enjoy what's left of what is turning out to be a pretty special Christmas Day.'

'There are still presents to unwrap,' Connor reminded us, and Owen told him, 'We'd better get a move on then, hadn't we?'

It felt quite like old times as we all worked together to get the table cleared and then the kitchen tidied. Very soon the dishwasher was humming and everyone was chatting easily. I felt myself relax, probably for the first time that day, and looked forward to the kind of family evening that, with all the upheaval the recent changes had wrought, I had been beginning to think would be lost to us forever.

As the table was laid out again, this time with all the traditional Christmas favourites – savouries such as sliced ham and turkey, assorted cheeses, crusty bread, various pickles and sausage rolls, together with an iced cake, mince pies, and a Yule log – we lit candles and placed them around the room.

It was only then that I noticed how dark it was getting outside and went to close the blinds. I had reached for the cord of the one across the French doors in the sitting room, when I paused as something caught my eye, and threw the doors wide open instead.

'Come and see this,' I called. 'It's snowing, and has been for some time by the look of it.'

I was very nearly bowled over as everyone rushed into the garden, and Owen reached out to steady me. We stood together, Owen's arm lightly draped around my shoulders, thoroughly enjoying the sight of all our children from the eldest to the youngest forgetting they were now adults and joining in a snowball fight.

Eventually, when everyone was very wet, Connor suggested making a snowman. That idea was met with great enthusiasm.

'You're all going to catch your death.' I laughed and urged them, 'Come and get out of those wet clothes and we'll have supper. You can do it later, or at Owen's tomorrow. This snow isn't going anywhere for a day or two yet if I'm any judge.'

'I'd better go and get Arthur,' Owen said, turning to go inside, with me right behind him. 'He'll be wondering what's happened to us.'

Then we heard Gizmo barking frantically.

Fourteen

Every one of us stopped to listen. The barking went on and on and to my ears the little dog was sounding more and more hysterical.

'It's definitely coming from the front of the house,' Jake decided.

'We'd best get round there.' Owen quickly made his way through the house with me hot on his heels and everyone else close behind.

I had an awful feeling I knew what we were going to find and was absolutely horrified to be proved right. Arthur had obviously been making his own way over to join us, but hadn't even made it as far as the gate before he came to grief in the snow and we discovered him lying, groaning a little, on the garden path.

Pointless to tell him he should have stayed put. Pointless to wish I had never noticed the snow that had distracted us all into forgetting the old man waiting, probably with increasing impatience, for someone to come and collect him.

'Oh, Arthur,' was all I could find to say.

'I'll be all right in a jiffy, Evie,' he assured me, already struggling to get to his feet.

'Don't move, Arthur, whatever you do,' Owen instructed, 'because we don't know what damage you've done to yourself and you may make matters worse. Jake, use your mobile to phone for an ambulance. The rest of you go and get blankets or a quilt and a pillow or cushion for Arthur's head – and for God's sake take that dog indoors with you.'

I was so glad for his calm good sense, because I was shaking like a leaf, probably more from shock than cold, I thought, as I knelt beside Arthur. I held his hand, encouraging him through chattering teeth to remain still, while assuring him that everything would be all right and the ambulance would soon be here.

'Oh, no, we don't want to be bothering the ambulance service on Christmas Day,' the old man was protesting, though his face was grey with pain. 'They'll have quite enough to do. Just help me up and get me inside. I shall be better presently.'

Connor came back very quickly with the quilt and pillow that Owen had requested; he also brought dry coats for Owen and me and made sure we put them on.

'From my, admittedly limited, experience I would say Arthur has probably fractured his hip,' he said quietly, his young face serious. 'I've told the girls to stay inside. It won't help to have them out here, blubbing all over the place.'

Thankfully it seemed no time at all before the blue flashing lights announced the arrival of the emergency vehicle and we all stood back as the very efficient male and female team took over – extremely grateful for their calm efficiency.

They spoke to Arthur clearly, asking him his name and introducing themselves to him. He managed to assure them he had not collapsed, but had lost his footing in the snow. I heard him say he was quite certain he had not banged his head or lost consciousness at all, not even for a minute, though his head and neck were still checked thoroughly. He was able to state clearly that the pain was at the top of his left thigh on the outside, which seemed to bear out what Connor had said.

The priority appeared to be getting Arthur up off the snowy ground as quickly as possible and into the warm ambulance. The tail lift on the vehicle was lowered in readiness and more equipment brought. From what I could hear and see Arthur was being asked if he had any allergies, and then he was given gas and air through a mouthpiece, encouraged and instructed by the young lady. Meanwhile the man worked around Arthur preparing the stretcher, then he was quickly lifted, moaning slightly and gritting his teeth, onto the stretcher, which was lifted and locked at waist height and wheeled to the waiting ambulance.

'Will someone be coming with him?' the young lady asked When I stepped forward she asked me to wait, then followed Arthur into the back of the ambulance.

By the time I was allowed inside and reminded to use the seatbelt before we set off, Arthur already had various devices attached to finger, arm and wrist and a screen close by was providing readings. I sat quite stunned and still shivering, but impressed by the speed of things, as the ambulance pulled away and one of the paramedics set to work completing what looked like an awful lot of paperwork.

Arthur was whisked away the minute we reached the

emergency department at the hospital. I made my way to the reception desk to see if the young woman behind it needed any details from me. When Owen arrived I had never been so glad to see anyone in my life.

'Arthur will be all right. He will won't he, Owen?' I practically threw myself at him, gripping the front of his coat with icy fingers, desperate to be reassured.

'I'm sure he will be.' Owen's tone was firm and he took my hands into the warmth of his own. 'He's a tough old bird, you know.'

'But he was in so much pain.' Tears trickled down my cheeks and I had never felt more useless.

'Jake seems pretty certain he's broken his hip, just as Connor thought. That's the danger at Arthur's age. Why the hell didn't I go round for him sooner?'

Owen sounded so cross with himself that I hastened to assure him, 'It wasn't your fault. I was the one distracting everyone. I should have remembered he was waiting.'

By the time we left the hospital, having sat a while with a philosophical Arthur, feeling the relief that he was at least in safe hands and the enormous guilt that we had allowed such a thing to happen to him, the dawn was breaking. With Owen driving carefully, we took in the beauty of the snowy scenery around us.

'So pretty and so treacherous,' Owen observed.

'Arthur wasn't the only one to end up in hospital last night. It was non-stop, wasn't it? He will be all right, won't he?' I couldn't stop fretting about Arthur, destined for surgery, and wondered what the dangers might be at his age.

'He'll be fine. The boys will be able to reassure you – especially about the aftercare.'

'Oh, yes, they'll know about that, because he'll require physiotherapy once the hip has been replaced, won't he? I believe the operation is very common.'

'Especially in the elderly,' Owen said ruefully. 'We should have taken better care of him.'

I almost reminded him that Arthur was my neighbour, not his, and therefore was my responsibility, but then I thought how nice it was that he was so willing to share the blame and how like him.

I couldn't believe that everyone was still up, fully clothed, waiting for news when we got home. I'd expected them all to be in bed and fast asleep long since. They had kept the heating on – and probably the kettle as well because tea was made in no time – and then they gathered round, impatient to hear the verdict on Arthur's injuries and to offer their thoughts on his chances of a full recovery.

'I've seen people of all ages up and walking in days after that op,' Jake said knowledgeably. 'Of course it depends on the person, but Arthur is the sort to do exactly as he's told. He'll want to be mobile again as soon as possible and do everything he can to make it happen.'

'They won't keep him in hospital any longer than necessary, either,' Connor agreed. 'What will you do about the dog?'

We all looked at Gizmo who, after the initial excitement of greeting Owen and me, had settled on my lap and was sleeping peacefully.

'I'll keep him here. I have Arthur's key and can go round

in the morning for his bits and pieces.' Then I laughed a little hollowly. 'Of course, it's morning already, so we should probably get what sleep we can. I'll see if he will settle on my bed.'

'Can we all stay here?' Alice asked. 'I'm so tired I could sleep on the floor.'

I managed a rueful smile and said, 'I don't think it will come to that, love. You can share with me, and Jake can share with Connor, but I'm afraid that leaves you with the couch, Owen.'

'Fine by me,' Owen rubbed his eyes, yawned and ordered, 'Right you lot, get off my bed.'

With Gizmo settled by our feet Alice and I were both asleep in no time and when I woke the sun was streaming through the window. Alice was still out for the count, though the dog stirred when I did, so not wishing him to disturb her, I quickly pulled a dressing gown on over my nightdress and went to let him out.

Owen was already busy in the kitchen, working as he often had at home, bare-chested, dressed only in his jeans and with no shoes or socks on his feet. As soon as he saw me he popped bacon under the grill, saying, 'I hope you're starving, because I am.'

'Absolutely, just give me time to let this dog outside and then lead me to it. No sign of anybody else yet?'

'Soundo. Alice?'

'Ditto. I think it will be some time before anyone stirs.' I laughed at the little dog's antics in the snow. 'Come and look, Owen. He wants to play but he's not very keen on getting his feet wet.'

Owen looked over my shoulder and we both laughed as the dog rushed between our legs and back into the house.

'He's obviously had enough for now. The snow's lovely with the sun on it, isn't it? It won't last long as the day warms up, though.' He turned round. 'Where did Gizmo go? I was going to cut a bit of bacon up in small pieces for him.'

'I wouldn't be surprised if he hasn't gone back to bed,' I guessed. Sure enough, when I checked he was already asleep curled at Alice's feet and looking very contented.

I reported back to Owen and watched him crack eggs into the frying pan. 'Do I have time to ring the hospital?' I asked.

'I already have,' Owen said. 'To start with they were extremely reluctant to tell me anything until I pointed out that we're not just Arthur's neighbours, but close friends who had actually phoned the ambulance and then come into hospital with him last night. When they still hesitated I explained that his only family live in Australia and we're all he has in this country. I gave the impression that we were husband and wife.' He shrugged, 'it just seemed easier.'

'And...?'

'And they still didn't tell me much, except that he's comfortable, and we can go and see him later.'

That was good enough for me. I was actually starving, which was hardly surprising since not so much as a biscuit had passed my lips since lunch the day before. As Owen ushered me to the table my mouth was already watering copiously and I set about the food placed in front of me with a will.

It felt exactly like old times, especially with the five children all sleeping under the same roof. In fact, it was *exactly* like old times I thought with a contented smile, because the only thing that had changed was the venue and this was just what I had hoped for when Owen and I first set the plans in motion to go our separate ways. We were a family – always would be – and get-togethers like this, though obviously we would wish for happier circumstances, should be a common occurrence. They were what family life was all about.

We ate pretty much in silence, enjoying every mouthful. When the plates were empty Owen made toast and we didn't hesitate before tucking into that as well, but now the edge had been taken off our appetites we found time to talk about the other subject on our minds, besides Arthur and his accident.

'What do you really think about Alice and Jake getting involved in a relationship?' Owen looked into my eyes, his placid demeanour encouraging an honest answer.

I shrugged and said firmly, 'I honestly have no problem with it as long as they are both quite sure of their feelings. Do you? I don't think they are doing anything wrong.'

I thought Owen looked relieved. 'Neither do I. We can easily check the legalities of a relationship between them on Google. The only reason I didn't rush off and do just that immediately was because I didn't want to give the impression that I was concerned – and because Arthur's accident then distracted me.'

'Same here.' I nodded. 'And of course, it is still early days and could turn out to be nothing serious.'

'I rather think it is serious, on Jake's part, at least,' Owen said. 'Have you seen the way he looks at Alice? I think it's safe to say he absolutely adores her – and he probably has for some time.'

'She's not the easiest of people, but then Jake obviously knows that, and he has always been very good with her.'

The telephone rang then, and several more calls in quick succession. The news about Arthur's accident seemed to have spread round the close like wild fire; I seemed to recall seeing a couple of people standing on the pavement when I climbed into the ambulance, and there were messages of goodwill to be passed on. Offers of help were made, which I knew I might be glad of when Arthur came home.

I'd just put down the phone when the doorbell rang, I went to answer it just as Owen stepped into the hall, obviously intent on doing the same thing.

Finding Stuart on the step was the last thing I'd expected, and then it dawned on me that it was already Boxing Day and we had arranged to spend it together.

I clapped a hand to my mouth. 'Oh, my God! Stuart, I'm so sorry. I completely forgot you were coming with everything that's happened. We've been....'

'Yes, Evie,' he looked from me in my dressing gown, to Owen, dressed only in his jeans, 'I can see what you've been and don't – just *don't* – insult my intelligence by telling me it's not what it seems.'

Fifteen

I was left looking at two sets of footprints on the snow-covered garden path, one coming up the path to my front door and one going the other way. It wasn't difficult to work out that Stuart would have seen a pathway with a pristine covering of snow as clear proof that Owen had stayed the night and then had drawn his own conclusions.

'I'll go after him.' Owen was already struggling into his coat. 'He's obviously got completely the wrong idea.'

'You and he seem to have *that* in common, if nothing else,' I said wryly, subtly reminding him of the times after I'd moved in when it had been Owen storming off in a huff because Stuart was in my house in what appeared to be compromising circumstances. 'Don't bother, Owen. I'll talk to him when he's calmed down. We don't need two of you rushing off in these conditions or there'll be another accident. Anyway,' I indicated his bare feet, 'you don't have any shoes on.'

I was determined not to let what had just happened become common knowledge and spoil the day for the chil-

NOT WHAT IT SEEMS

dren. They only had a few more days left of a festive break from challenging jobs and university courses and had already been upset enough by Arthur's unfortunate accident. I wasn't going to let a stupid misunderstanding and the childish behaviour of one person – who, I reminded myself, was supposed to be an adult and wasn't even family – cast another shadow. That's what I told Owen as sounds of the rest of the household rousing themselves reached our ears.

I showered and dressed in jeans and a warm sweater as Owen took over in the kitchen yet again and set about feeding the family. While they were eating I popped round and let myself into Arthur's house. It took no time to gather up Gizmo's bed, bowls, brush and food, then I quickly found nightwear, a towel, toiletries and anything I thought Arthur might need for a stay in hospital. I also found his son's contact details by the phone and took that with me as well.

The house was as neat and tidy as you would expect from the obvious effort that Arthur always took with his own appearance, so there was nothing to be done, apart from checking that the back door and all the windows were secure. I returned to join my family for more tea and toast and to listen to their plans for the day ahead.

Obviously, my original intention of spending the day with Stuart was a non-starter, because what with Arthur's accident and Stuart jumping to wrong conclusions everything was a bit up in the air.

'I believe you did have your own plans for today, Mum,' Alice reminded me with absolutely no hint of criticism in her tone. 'But I expect you might have to revise them, with Arthur being in hospital and you wanting to spent time there with him. You know you're more than welcome to join us all at Owen's at any point today.'

Everyone else at the table, including Owen warmly endorsed this. He also gave it as his intention to go with me to visit Arthur. 'For one thing,' he said, 'I wouldn't be happy for you to be out driving in these conditions – and yes,' he added, putting up his hand, 'I do know you are a very careful driver, but there is a lot of snow out there and the four by four has a better grip. Anyway, I'd like to see Arthur myself,' he added, 'if you don't mind.

'Now,' he continued, 'I'll also be taking the rest of you across to mine as soon as you're ready and please don't waste time arguing. It's not that I don't trust you, just as it's not that I don't trust Evie, but you won't be the only ones on the road, and a lot of them will be driving like complete idiots. I have the experience required to avoid them. Just put it down to a father being over-protective.'

The protestations that were about to be uttered were immediately silenced and I really wanted to hug Owen for being – well, Owen.

'Thank you,' I mouthed at him over the children's heads, and he shrugged and smiled at me. 'Don't worry about clearing up,' I told everyone firmly as they made moves to do just that, 'I won't be going anywhere until visiting time. At two, isn't it, Owen?'

They needed no further telling and there was the usual flurry as Connor and the girls rushed round gathering what they classed as essential for the day.

'There are still presents under the tree,' Ella pointed out. 'Shall we take them with us?'

'Good idea.' I paused in the act of stacking the dishwasher and handed her a carrier bag from the ones I kept in the cupboard, and added, 'Don't forget to take all the leftover meat and pickles from yesterday. Even Gizmo won't want to be eating turkey forever.'

The silence after they all left was so deafening that I had to put the radio on. I thought how quickly you could get used to the noise and bustle of family life again. I picked up scattered garments and delivered them to the correct guest room, automatically straightening duvets and plumping up pillows as I went. The little dog was always right behind me and I found I liked knowing he was there.

'Fancy a walk,' I asked him when I was all done, and he skipped around my feet, obviously recognizing the key word. 'Shame you haven't got any of these,' I told him as I tugged a pair of rarely worn wellingtons onto my feet.

It wasn't actually as bad out there as I had feared; because once we were away from the cul-de-sac most of the roads and the pavements seemed to have been treated and had also seen a fair bit of traffic, either from vehicles or people on foot. The bit of sun, weak as it was, was also doing its best to melt the snow and the result was mainly slush spread thinly and diminishing by the minute.

Gizmo was very well behaved and I found I really enjoyed the novelty of walking a dog. It was surprisingly busy on the streets for Boxing Day and Gizmo was so cute that people often stopped me to pet him and ask what breed he was. There were others, who obviously knew Arthur, stopping me to enquire after him and they were horrified to hear what had happened to him. I promised time and again to pass their best to him, without any idea at all who most of them might be.

The park I eventually came to seemed as busy as the streets, yet the snow was not as trampled in some areas, especially on the grass. There were children building snowmen, engaged in snowball fights and being pulled along on toboggans. There were any number of other dog-walkers, too. I soon found myself surrounded and, as I explained why I came to be walking Gizmo, others came to join in. Arthur was obviously a very popular man and everyone was eager to help in any way they could.

'Are you all right looking after the dog for him?' a young lady asked, adding, 'I'd be quite happy to take him home with Poppy.' She rested her hand on the head of a very handsome Boxer dog. 'They are great friends despite their very dissimilar sizes.'

'I'm enjoying having him around,' I assured her, 'But thank you for the offer, it's very kind of you.'

Owen was waiting on the doorstep when I got back. I immediately regretted the meanness that had caused me to refuse to offer him a key. He was my best friend, for heaven's sake, and was hardly going to suddenly start to take liberties.

I handed him one, saying, 'For emergencies and situations such as this.'

'Of course,' he agreed, adding it to his key ring with no further comment.

'We've probably got time for a sandwich – if the children have left anything in the fridge.'

I made a move to check, but Owen laughed and said, 'Thanks, but no thanks, Evie. I'm still full of breakfast.'

I smiled back and admitted, 'Me, too, really. I was being greedy. I just need to look for an overnight bag and another one that isn't too feminine for Arthur's toiletries. He probably has both but I didn't like to poke around among his things too much.'

'What on earth could a man of his advanced years have to hide?' Owen looked amused.

'We're all entitled to our secrets – whatever age we may be,' I reminded him firmly. 'I won't be a minute.'

I've never been keen on driving in adverse weather conditions and had reason to be grateful for Owen's insistence on driving me to the hospital when at one point the driver in front braked suddenly for no apparent reason and Owen managed to stop only millimetres from his bumper.

Both of my feet jammed to the floor in a fruitless search for a brake and the overnight bag slid gracefully from my lap to the floor. Owen's arm had been flung instinctively in front of me, but the seat belt had locked in place and held me firm. Without it I would certainly have been thrown forward and probably hit the windscreen. Had I been the one driving I had no doubt I'd have been ringing for a breakdown truck once I'd got over the shock of the collision that would undoubtedly have taken place.

'Idiot,' Owen muttered. I greatly admired his restraint.

The multi-storey car park was already incredibly busy even though there was a little while to go before visiting hours started. We joined the queue that crawled from level to level until someone obligingly pulled out in front of us and

Owen nipped briskly into the space before anyone could beat us to it.

I would guess that Arthur had been given plenty of pain relief because he seemed quite perky when we reached his bedside. He told us the operation was scheduled for the next day. Supported by pillows, he was wearing a most unflattering hospital gown, but he assured us he was being well taken care of and even praised the food. Probably looked on it as a bonus that he didn't have to cook it – I knew I would have done.

I went through the contents of the overnight and toiletry bags in case there was anything I might have missed and was pleased that I seemed to have brought everything he might need. It was when he mentioned Ron that I clapped a hand over my mouth and admitted that, though I had thought to pick up his number, I had yet to ring him.

'I'll do it as soon as I get home,' I promised.

'They're about eleven hours in front of us,' Owen reminded me. 'It will be the middle of the night.'

'Don't worry, Evie.' Arthur patted my hand. 'What he doesn't know can't worry him. Let him enjoy his Christmas for a bit longer and then be sure to tell him that I'm fine. You could do it on my Skype if I give you my passwords, to save your phone bill.'

'I'll ring him tomorrow,' I decided. 'It might give him more of a shock if a strange face pops up on your Skype.'

After assuring Arthur that Gizmo was just fine staying with me, and passing on the many encouraging messages from people that he seemed to recognize from my descriptions, we took our leave.

'I didn't like to say so in front of Arthur,' Owen said, as we drove from the car park, 'but he will need some kind of after-care besides physio when he's discharged from the hospital. He may not be capable of living on his own for a while.'

I nodded. 'Yes, I'd already thought of that. He'll have to come and stay with me.'

'He's not really your responsibility, Evie,' was the reminder.

'Who else does he have?'

'Well, when you put it like that. I'd like to help in any way I can if you'll let me.' He saw my look and added, 'I know, he's not my responsibility, either, but he's a nice old chap. I've become fond of him, too.'

'I think we all have. I'll talk to the nursing staff once he's had his operation and find out what's involved.'

He nodded, then changed the subject. 'Are you coming home with me? We'd all like you to be there.'

'What about Gizmo?'

'You shouldn't even need to ask, Evie. We'll stop by and pick him up on the way.'

I thought about the very different plans I'd made to be with Stuart for the day, but the thought was fleeting. I was quite sure he wouldn't have been prepared to hang around for most of the day while I visited Arthur – even if he hadn't got the wrong end of the stick about Owen and me and stormed off. I reminded myself quite sternly that I was very lucky to have an alternative offer which would give me more time to enjoy my family.

'Thank you.'

'I feel to blame for your misunderstanding with…'

'Stuart,' I finished for him. 'Well, you're not to blame in any way. Please don't give it another thought because I shan't.'

We decided to give Gizmo a quick walk before setting off again. The snow was melting rapidly now, leaving little piles of slush and numerous puddles for the unwary to step into, although I thought the park still looked quite pretty in places where the snow still lay white on the grass especially under the shade of the trees.

The quick walk took a little longer than we'd expected because of the number of times we were stopped for news of Arthur. It was getting quite late before we were on our way again.

'Thank goodness,' Alice greeted us. 'What on earth took you so long? We were getting worried.'

'Getting worried and getting hungry,' Connor put in and was immediately told to 'shush' by the others.

'Don't tell me you haven't eaten,' I said, making my way through to the kitchen.

One glance at the buffet so beautifully set out in the limited space available – obviously untouched – confirmed that they had been patiently waiting all this time so that we could all eat together.

'It wouldn't have seemed right to start without you,' Jake explained, ushering us both to the table.

'Help yourselves and then take your plate through to the sitting room,' Ella encouraged. 'We'll have to eat on our laps because there's not enough room or enough chairs in here. We can always come back for second helpings.'

Very soon there was silence as we tucked into plates

loaded with cold meats and pickles accompanied by crusty bread thickly spread with butter. It was clear that we were all absolutely starving – it *had* been a very long time since breakfast – but as soon as the edge had been taken off their appetites the questions started.

'How is Arthur?'

'When is his operation?'

'How long will he be in hospital?'

Jake, as a qualified physiotherapist, and Connor, two years into his course to qualify in the same field, were able to talk knowledgeably about the aftercare he could expect. Both agreed he would need help at home, particularly given his age.

After making a great show of forcing ourselves to enjoy trifle, mince pies and various other treats, Ella, Mai and Connor begged to be able to take Gizmo for another walk. Alice and Jake insisted on clearing away and washing up.

'Put your feet up and enjoy another glass of wine, Mum,' Alice said with a smile. 'You've been rushing about all day.'

'Actually, I would really love a nice cup of tea.'

'Me, too,' Owen agreed, stretching his feet out in front of the real fire that was burning in the grate and wiggling his toes in the way he had been doing ever since I first knew him.

When I looked at him again he was sound asleep. I hoped they would hurry up with that tea or I had the feeling I would be joining him. A soft tap at the front door roused me from a very comfortable reverie and brought my head up, though Owen slept peacefully on.

Alice put her head round the kitchen door. Holding up

rubber-gloved hands covered in soap suds, she said, 'Could you get that, Mum? It's probably the rest of them back from their walk.'

I was surprised they didn't have a key between them, but then I supposed there was no reason they should because they were all staying at my place this holiday.

'Wipe your feet,' I warned. I had already begun to turn away when I realized that the lone person standing on the step was Stuart.

Sixteen

I turned back and stared at Stuart. He stared back at me, then he held his hands, palms up, in a gesture of supplication, saying in a deeply apologetic tone, 'I think it's actually you who should be wiping your feet – all over me.'

'Well,' I said in a hard, flat tone without a hint of forgiveness, 'you won't find me disagreeing with that. What are you doing here?'

'I telephoned your house this morning. I think you had gone round to Arthur's house or something. I spoke to your daughter – or it could have been your stepdaughter – and she explained what had happened. I felt really bad about my behaviour and said so. It was her idea for me to call round and apologize in person. I'm really so sorry for jumping to stupid conclusions, Evie, especially after seeing the other guy do exactly the same a couple of times. I'm also very sorry indeed to hear about Arthur's accident. He's such a nice old boy.'

'You coming here to apologize would have meant more if it hadn't taken someone else to point out that you *were* jumping to conclusions,' I told him, quite ready to turn him away. 'I know what it must have looked like, but couldn't you just have asked what was happening – and then waited for the answer?'

'Yes, I could. Sorry,' he said again.

'Aren't you going to invite Stuart in?'

Alice appeared beside me. I had no doubt she was the one who had answered the phone and had then decided to take matters into her own hands without so much as a by-your-leave. She was looking immensely pleased with what amounted to the result of her interference.

It was clear she thought she had done something wonderful for me, especially in the light of her previous disapproval; that was the only thing that stopped me from turning Stuart away and giving her an abrupt warning not to interfere in my life in the future. Without a word I stood aside. Stuart came inside to join a family gathering that was never intended to include him.

Owen woke with a start from what must have been a very deep sleep. If he was annoyed to find that an interloper had joined the ranks while he slept, he hid it extremely well.

Alice introduced Jake, then took him off to the kitchen on the pretext of making sandwiches that nobody was going to want to eat. I think she'd have liked Owen to join them, but he was oblivious to her hints and then Connor, Ella and Mai arrived back with Gizmo, so there was no chance at all of a cosy tête-à-tête.

I was pleased that the children insisted on playing charades – just as we always had done on Boxing Night – despite the presence of an outsider. To his credit Stuart joined in with a convincing show of enthusiasm, and if I noticed a distinct edge of competitiveness between him and Owen, I doubt anyone else did. However, I did draw the line at then watching a fight for supremacy over the Monopoly board. I gathered my things and Gizmo, together and stated my intention to return home.

'It's a bit early,' Connor protested.

'You don't have to come. I'm sure Stuart won't mind giving me a lift home and then Owen can bring the rest of you later. We all had lifts with Owen,' I explained to Stuart, 'because he doesn't trust a single one of us to drive in the snow.'

Owen protested, but Stuart just said, 'Very sensible. It's mostly gone now, but I've seen a good few shunts around the area today. Not worth taking the chance if you don't have to.'

We drove most of the way in near silence, and what comments were made were stilted to say the least. It wasn't until Stuart had pulled his vehicle across my driveway and I was reaching for the door handle with an abrupt, 'Good night, thanks for the lift,' that he put out his hands in a carbon copy of his earlier supplicating gesture.

'OK, OK, I overreacted, Evie. You might even have done the same yourself, faced with a similar scenario. I was as jealous as hell, and I freely admit it.'

I turned in my seat and gave him a straight look. 'You could have just trusted me, Stuart. I know you haven't known me long, but you must know I'm not the sort of person to sleep around.'

'You've shared a house, a family and a life with the guy for years – I would hardly call that sleeping around.'

'Well, I would. I'm sure I've said this to you before, probably more than once, but I'll say it again anyway, we shared a house, *not* a bed. Not ever, not even once. I've spent practically my whole life explaining this, and if it's something I am going to be continually doing for your peace of mind then we have to forget this.' I paused and searched unsuccessfully for a word to explain the 'this' that Stuart and I shared and ended up saying, 'us', then adding, 'if there is an us.'

'You must know there is.' Stuart reached to take my hand, 'I want to be the only man in your life – and in your bed, too, when the time is right – but I understand that you have a long history with Owen. I'm doing my very best to accept that and trying come to terms with it. Honestly.'

He sounded so humble that I felt the tension seeping out of me; and some of the warmth I'd felt towards him since our first meeting began to return.

'Do you want to come in?' I offered.

'Yes, please, if that's OK with you.'

I gathered up my bag and the dog from the back seat and leaving Stuart to follow, I let myself into the house. By the time we'd watched a DVD that made us laugh and I'd drunk a bottle of wine which Stuart did little more than taste I had started to feel comfortable with him again and even welcomed his tentative advances. In fact, things were starting to warm up nicely, when the front door opened and Ella could be heard protesting loudly about Connor's competitive streak when it came to board games.

'You don't *always* have to win,' she was saying indignantly, as Stuart and I quickly moved apart, fastened buttons and generally tidied our ruffled appearance. I just hoped we weren't looking too flushed.

'I thought winning was the whole point.' He was shrugging as he came in the door, then, eyeing the bottle on the coffee table, he forgot the conversation he was having to enquire, 'Any wine left, Mum?'

'Afraid not,' I said with a smile, 'but get another bottle from the fridge if you like, and some more glasses.'

'You'll have a hangover in the morning,' Mai warned.

'I'm on holiday,' he pointed out with a grin, and bringing the fresh bottle to the table, offered to replenish our glasses.

'Not for me,' Stuart said immediately, getting up. 'I really should be getting off. I've got work tomorrow.'

'So soon?' I said.

'It's what comes of being self-employed,' he told me ruefully, as I walked with him to the front door. Then he suggested, 'Perhaps we can get together at the weekend and make up for the date we missed out on through my stupidity.'

'Erm, sorry, but these three kids are all going back to uni this weekend, and I want to be around to see them off.'

To his credit Stuart made an effort to hide the fact that he was disgruntled at my refusal. That he didn't understand my reason for it became clear when he pointed out, 'Hardly kids, are they?'

'To me they are and it might be a while before I see them again. Perhaps we can meet up for a drink one evening?'

'I'll ring you,' he said abruptly, but then he scooped me up in his arms and kissed me until I was breathless and we were both pretty aroused.

As I closed the door behind him I was confused – very confused.

'Another glass of wine?' Connor wagged the bottle at me.

I shook my head. 'Not for me, I'm off to bed.'

'Me, too,' Mai said, stretching and yawning, 'it's almost midnight.'

I glanced at the clock, and as I did so I suddenly said, 'How far in front is Australian time to ours?'

'Didn't I hear someone say it was eleven hours?' Ella supplied helpfully.

'Right.' I made up my mind. 'I'm going to ring Arthur's son, so can you all keep the noise down, please?'

'We aren't making any noise,' Connor pointed out.

'Well, don't start,' I advised, going into the hall for the number I wanted and the telephone receiver.

The male voice that answered was pleasantly deep with a very distinctive Australian accent, as might have been expected. The line was so clear he could have been in the next street.

'Am I speaking to Ron Parkinson?' I began hesitantly; when he confirmed that he was I hurried on: 'You won't know me, but I live next door to your dad.'

'Actually, I do feel as if I know you,' he replied, and I could hear the smile in his voice. 'You must be Evie. My dad talks about you all the time; he seems to be very fond of you.'

'And I am of him, but—'

'Is something wrong?' His voice sharpened.

'Arthur has had an accident.' I heard the intake of his breath and hurried to say, 'He's fine, really. Well, he *is* in hospital and his hip *is* broken, but he's in no danger and will be fine. He slipped in the snow on Christmas Night.'

I gave him the details of the hospital and did my best to

assure him that I was quite happy to take care of Arthur when he came home with his new hip. Eventually, I replaced the phone on its stand, went back into the sitting room and collapsed on the couch.

'I think I'll have that glass of wine now,' I told Connor, 'if there's any left.'

'Was he very cross about it being our fault he fell?' Connor asked as he poured it.

'On the contrary, he doesn't blame us in the slightest and is grateful for everything we've done for Arthur.'

'Oh. Only you looked a bit shocked when you came in, and I thought he might have had a go at you – at us.' The two girls nodded in agreement and they all looked at me anxiously.

'If I look shocked it's because Ron – Arthur's son – has said that he'll be coming over with his family just as soon as they can get a flight. He said he had just been given the timely reminder he needed of his father's advanced years and, as good though Skype is, at times like this it isn't nearly good enough.'

What I didn't mention to the children was that his words had brought uncomfortable and very unwelcome thoughts of my own parents and their respective ages – and though I pushed those thoughts away with grim determination, they came back again and again throughout a very long and sleepless night.

I had no trouble at all keeping busy the next day. Up at first light, I was in the park with Gizmo before any of my guests had so much as raised an eyelid. When I got back I delivered cups of tea to their bedsides, along with the reminder that dirty washing needed to find its way into the laundry now if it was to be washed, dried and ironed by the weekend.

While they were still groaning, I made my way round to Arthur's and viewed the bungalow with a critical eye before stripping Arthur's bed and making it up with fresh bedding that I found in the airing cupboard. I wondered how his Australian family were going to manage about sleeping arrangements because there was only the one bed, before reminding myself that it was none of my business and setting to with the duster, polish and vacuum. Dust had barely had time to settle in the short time Arthur had been absent, but I felt I should be doing something.

I took the replaced bedding home with me, along with a few bits and pieces I'd discovered in the laundry basket tucked into the corner of the bathroom, and was more than ready for the mug of tea and the freshly made bacon sand-wiches I found waiting for me.

I had my sleeves rolled up and piles of dirty laundry scat-tered everywhere when the doorbell rang, making me tut under my breath at the unwelcome interruption.

It was Ruth, one half of the posh couple from the bungalow on the other side of me from Arthur's, looking immaculate as ever in black trousers and a black top with a tiny bit of sparkle evident, probably as a nod to the festive season.

'My word, you do look busy, Evelyn,' she said in her precise way, but I noticed that she had dropped the haughty tone since the pre-Christmas get-together. 'I won't keep you, but I just thought I would call to ask if you have any news of Arthur?'

I pushed my untidy hair self-consciously back from my face and hoped I didn't have grease down my top from the bacon sandwich.

'Excuse the mess,' I said, 'but the children are going back to their various universities this weekend and they seem to have suddenly discovered that every garment they brought with them needs washing. Arthur,' I continued, getting back to the point of her visit, 'should be having his operation this morning, and I'm to ring about midday. I've been in touch with his son and he's coming over from Australia as soon as he can.'

'Oh, I am pleased. He'll need family at a time like this – not that you haven't been wonderful. You've put us all to shame with your friendly ways, Evelyn. Your party has resulted in Giles and me and several others realizing how very antisocial we've always been with our neighbours in the close and we'd now like to throw one of our own – on New Year's Eve. I do hope you're free to come.'

'Oh, that would be great,' I said, and meant it.

'And bring that lovely man of yours,' she encouraged. 'Owen, wasn't it? I managed to have a quick word with him the night of Arthur's accident,' she added, seeing my curious look. 'He was in a rush to join you at the hospital but he still took the time to answer my questions with the most amazing patience. Do be sure to bring him with you, won't you?'

'I'll be sure to let Owen know that he's invited when I next see him,' I said, thereby making it abundantly clear that he didn't live with me and so wouldn't be brought to the party by me. I wasn't sure how I could also make it clear that he wasn't 'that lovely man of mine', without appearing rather churlish.

Connor came down the stairs at that moment with yet another armful of washing. Ruth gave me a sympathetic look and said, 'I'll leave you to get on, Evelyn. Please do give Arthur our very best and wish him well soon. I'll pass on the news of him round the close to save you being inundated with visitors.'

Within a very short time the house resembled a Chinese laundry, with washing draped over radiators and doors throughout. We gave the washing line a go as well, because even though it was still December with a very distinct chill in the air the stiff breeze might just do its stuff. For the very first time since the move I thought regretfully of the big house with its utility room and dryer and wondered if life really had been much simpler then.

Seventeen

After breaking off only to visit Arthur at the hospital during the afternoon, I was still ironing long after the children had gone out, at my urging, to meet their Brankstone friends at the local pub. To be fair, the two girls had done more than their fair share throughout the day and we had all been in agreement that to have Connor wielding a hot iron wasn't a good idea at all. Instead he had kept us constantly supplied with teas, coffees, soft drinks, snacks and even meals throughout the day.

Arthur had been surprisingly chipper and was extremely proud of the newly fitted hip which, he stated, was 'just grand'. The old one had, apparently given him gyp at times in damp weather – though I'd never once heard him complain – and he was glad to see the back of it.

He'd apparently been assured by the nurses that he would soon be walking miles without any problem; neither of us had any reason to doubt them. I didn't say a word to him about Ron's impending visit, at his son's request. I just hoped I would be there to see Arthur's face when he arrived out of the blue.

I was really going to miss Gizmo, I decided, looking at him lying on the rug with his head on his tiny paws, his bright little eyes following my every movement. I idly pondered on the advisability of getting a dog of my own as I pressed innumerable T-shirts one after the other and wondered if I was ever going to get to the bottom of the washing-basket.

With Gizmo at my heels I came in from the garden carrying the last armful of still damp washing and almost jumped out of my skin when I found Owen in the kitchen, putting the kettle on.

'I did ring the bell but I thought you were out walking the dog when I didn't hear him bark,' he said, laughing down at Gizmo as the tiny dog belatedly went into a frenzy of yapping around his feet. 'So I let myself in. I hope you don't mind. Cup of tea?'

'Thanks,' I accepted gratefully, too tired to be cross at his use of the key I'd given him for emergencies.

'Your house looks a lot like mine.' He indicated the neat piles of pressed clothes on every available surface. 'Don't any of them have launderettes where they live?'

I shook my head. 'Evidently not,' I said, and went back to my position behind the ironing board.

Owen budged a pile of clothes over with the edge of the tray, set it on the dining room table and offered, 'I could take over for a while, Evie. Sit down and enjoy your tea and tell me about Arthur. I'd have liked to visit him with you, but I had to price a couple of jobs this afternoon. I'll be glad of the work because, as you know, it usually goes quiet after Christmas, until everyone's paid their credit card bills off.'

I wasn't surprised by his offer of help, because it was

exactly how we had used to operate when we shared a house, dividing the housework evenly between us. I was grateful – though I did wonder what he was doing here and eventually had to ask.

He puffed out his cheeks and then admitted, 'Oh, Alice and Jake are bickering. To be honest they've hardly stopped all day and it's seriously beginning to get on my nerves.'

'Oh, dear,' I said, pouring tea out for us both and fetching my dwindling supply of biscuits. 'I don't think they have biscuits where they live either,' I commented, peering into the barrel.

'Oh, dear, indeed!' Owen didn't look up from the ironing board, where a blouse I recognized as mine was being conscientiously smoothed of all creases. 'It was either come here or go to bed early.'

'You could have gone to the pub and joined the others.'

'Mmm,' he said, without any interest, but then looked up and asked, 'You don't mind me coming here, do you?'

I grinned and the last trace of annoyance about the key left me. 'Well, I can hardly complain, can I? You always were much better at ironing than me.' He still didn't look sure, so I added, 'We're friends, aren't we? Always have been, probably always will be.'

'I hope so. Feel free any time to come over and do my ironing, by the way.'

'Thank you,' I said with mock gratitude. 'I'll be sure to take you up on that offer very soon.'

We spent a while discussing Arthur, his circumstances, and the fact that his son was arriving soon, then we returned to the subject of Alice and Jake's relationship.

'I suppose all couples bicker,' I thought out loud, adding, 'I'm sure we must have – and we weren't even a proper couple.'

'Did we?' Owen looked surprised. 'I always thought we got along absolutely great. Much better than most of the conventional couples we knew. Sandy and James were a complete nightmare – and they very probably still are. From what I remember of them, they would start a quarrel over the most ridiculous things.'

'Whether tomatoes should be sliced or chopped in a salad,' I recalled, with the same sense of amazement I'd felt at the time. 'Remember that? They almost came to blows over that one, until we suggested they just got cherry tomatoes and served them whole.'

'Knocker or bell for their front door – that was another one – and it raged on for ages, until I fitted both just to shut them up.'

I nodded. 'That stopped them in their tracks. You have both knocker and bell as well now, thanks to my generosity, and I hope you have the bell set up to play 'Auld Lang Syne', with the New Year looming. Oh, yes, and we've both been invited to my next door neighbours' New Year's Eve party, if you're interested. I have to say Ruth seems *very* taken with you since apparently speaking to you on the night of Arthur's accident and she has *particularly* asked me to be sure to mention it to you.

'Joking aside, though, Owen,' I became suddenly serious, 'I was cross – and I mean *really* cross – that Sandy went out of her way to tell our children I was seeing someone. I probably *should* have mentioned it to them sooner, but in my defence

Stuart and I had barely even been on a proper date at that point. *You* wouldn't even have known about us if you hadn't bumped into us in the supermarket on the same night as Sandy saw us. You didn't rush off to share the news, yet you had far more right than she did to get involved. I only wanted to tell the children together. We both know what they're like, Owen. You tell one of them *anything* on the phone and before you can reach the rest they've all texted each other.'

'Yes, but then Sandy always did think she knew best,' was Owen's very honest opinion.

'You're *so* right.' I stared at him. 'She would never have it that we weren't a match made in heaven, destined to be together forever, and go on to have even more children together. I remember she used to question me very closely about our sleeping arrangements, and quite clearly didn't believe that we weren't nipping across the landing on a regular basis. I actually had to put her in her place more than once.'

'You, too?' Owen grimaced. 'Still, they did us a kindness just by introducing us to each other. The last few years could have been very different – even impossible for us both – without the working arrangement we came up with that really did work. There,' he put the last neatly pressed item onto the correct pile, and began to fold up the ironing board. 'All done,' he said, and then asked, 'You don't fancy joining the gang at the pub, do you, Evie? I don't feel like going home yet and I won't feel like such an old duffer if you're with me.'

'Coward!' I laughed at him. 'How can I refuse since you've released me from the hell of seemingly endless ironing a lot sooner than I'd expected to finish. I'll get my coat.'

As it was just Owen and the local pub, I didn't feel the need to do more than change into a fresh T-shirt, brush my hair and tuck my jeans into a pair of boots. As an afterthought I swiped on a dab of lipstick, then grabbed my leather jacket, scarf and bag, and I was ready.

It wasn't far, so we walked arm in arm, chatting easily, and because this was something we had done so many times before while we shared a house it felt oddly as if time had stopped and nothing had changed. The feeling increased when we walked into the pub and were quickly encircled by our children and their friends.

The happy atmosphere changed considerably when Alice and Jake joined us soon after our own arrival. It was clear that the row Owen had mentioned was on-going and they were scarcely speaking. Though Jake was making an effort to behave normally and join in the general conversation, Alice had a face like thunder and was obviously intending to make no effort at all. I would have wondered why she had bothered to come out if I wasn't well aware that when Alice was upset she wanted everyone to know it.

I tried, Owen tried, Connor, Ella and Mai tried, and most of all Jake tried to coax her into a better mood, but it was all to no avail because she absolutely wasn't having any of it. The mellow feeling induced by the first glass of wine disappeared as I became more on edge and I stupidly drank more quickly in the hope of getting back to the same state. All I managed was to become quite drunk quite quickly, to the point that I found everything hysterically funny – even Alice's stony face.

'You,' she hissed, 'are a disgrace and just need to grow up.'

I was proud when I managed to say, very carefully, and without even the hint of a slur, 'I think, Alice that it is *you* who needs to grow up, actually, and to learn that the whole world does not revolve around *you.*'

With that I turned on a heel that seemed suddenly to have become very unstable. I made my way unsteadily to the door and shoved it open. When the cold air hit me I had to keep a firm hold on to the door handle until I got my bearings or I would have taken a nosedive down steps I hadn't even noticed on the way in. I was wondering in a vague kind of way how on earth I was going to manage the walk home when I felt a firm hand under my elbow and looked up into Owen's kind blue eyes.

I felt obliged to say, 'I'll be fine, honestly,' and prayed he wouldn't take his hand away.

'Of course you will,' he agreed, 'but I have to go back to yours to pick up my car, so we'd just as well walk together.'

Walking together consisted of me doing my best to put one foot in front of the other and hanging onto Owen for dear life. I was sober enough to feel pretty stupid and quite cross with myself. In the end I really felt I should apologize for the state I was in.

'So sorry,' I mumbled, keeping my gaze steadfastly on the pavement in front and wondering that the short walk to the pub appeared to have trebled itself for the return journey.

'Nothing to be sorry about – if I hadn't been driving I would happily have joined you.'

'I s'pose we could talk about it – about them and their relationship?'

'It won't help,' Owen said sensibly.

The relief when we turned the corner into my cul-de-sac was indescribable: I felt very little nearer to a sober state, though I managed a creditably normal, 'Good evening,' greeting to Giles, who was just getting out of his car.

I had enough sense to allow Owen to unlock the door, because I feared that trying to get a Yale key into such a tiny lock might prove to be embarrassing since it was bound to take several attempts. Gizmo rushed to meet us, then he was through the door and between our legs before either of us could do a single thing stop him.

'I'll catch him, you go on in,' Owen offered, but I remained on the step leaning against the doorframe and roaring with laughter at the dog's determined efforts to avoid capture. 'Got you, you little...' Owen said, once he had the animal safely tucked under one arm and me supported by the other. 'Trouble, you are, the pair of you,' he added as soon as he had managed to get us both inside and had shut the door firmly behind us. 'Now, could you just try and keep out of mischief while I put the kettle on.'

The coffee he put in front of me was so hot and so strong that the spoon could have stood up on its own. I shuddered as the bitter taste burned a trail down my throat but continued to sip with grim determination, feeling it was crucial that I should sober up so that Owen could get away.

'Funny,' Owen said, looking around, 'I could never have imagined us living separate lives, but it seems to be working quite well, doesn't it? The children have all taken it in their stride, I think, even Alice in the end. I expect once the New Year is over, and life gets back to normal you'll be getting down to that novel.'

'Erm, yes,' I agreed, realizing with a bit of a start that I had scarcely given it a thought since the day I'd moved house, despite the state-of-the-art office awaiting me upstairs.

The burning desire to get working on the plot I'd been carrying round in my head for more years than I cared to remember seemed to have deserted me somewhere along the way. I knew it was just an excuse, but there always seemed to be so much going on and it would probably need a good pair of bellows blasting ideas at me to get the spark of the original plot to burst into flames again.

The idea of writing a whole novel suddenly seemed very daunting even given my inebriated state, though I usually found that alcohol could be relied on to give a boost to my confidence. I suddenly realized that Owen was speaking to me and I forced myself to concentrate.

'I do admire you, Evie,' he was saying seriously, 'because although I know we always said we would move on once the children had all gone to university, left to me it wouldn't have happened. Now that you're dating again it's given me another massive push. You'll be pleased to hear that I've met someone as well, and, though it's early days, we get on really well, so we are planning to see a lot more of one another in the future.'

'Oh,' I said, 'that's great. That's really great. I'm *so* pleased.'

A sudden wave of nausea swept over me and I only just made it to the bathroom in time. I felt absolutely wretched and, staring into the mirror at my streaming eyes and chalk-white face, I told myself it just served me right. It *was* the alcohol, of course, and had absolutely *nothing* to do with Owen's news, because I couldn't have been more thrilled for him.

Eighteen

It felt as if my hangover was still raging days later when the children were packing their holdalls with freshly laundered clothes ready for the journey back to their own lives. I made a determined effort to convince myself I just had a touch of flu and was only feeling down because of that and the fact that I was going to miss them so much, but it didn't seem to be working particularly well.

We all went out for a family meal at our favourite Italian restaurant the night before they were leaving. On this occasion the atmosphere between Alice and Jake was showing at least some signs of a slight improvement and appeared merely chilly rather than demonstrating the extreme arctic iciness that they'd displayed previously. Alice did at least make a noticeable effort to be sociable and contribute to the general conversation, for which I was grateful, even if she did sit as far away from Jake as possible.

For some reason it really annoyed me when Owen waited for me to make my menu choices before he made his own – even though it was what he'd always done. I wondered irritably if it was a practice he would continue with his new woman and what she would make of a habit that could really be quite irritating at times. It would just serve him right, I thought with a touch of unusual asperity, if he continued the practice and discovered that her selections weren't at all to his taste.

'It's been a brilliant Christmas,' Ella said, 'apart from poor Arthur's accident.'

'Yes, thank you both so much for everything,' Mai agreed, 'and I don't just mean the presents, although they are fabulous.'

'Oh, yes.' Alice seemed to come out of a reverie that had appeared to be holding her attention for a while and she turned to me with a sudden bright smile that completely took me by surprise, so that I blinked. 'We forgot to give you your main present with everything that went on.'

'Like you throwing hissy fits everywhere,' I heard Connor mutter under his breath.

I threw him a warning look and said, 'But I've had lots of presents.'

'Not this one, Mum.' Alice looked pleased with herself as she drew a long white envelope from her bag and handed it to me with a mysterious and very satisfied smile.

I was expecting tickets for a show, if I was honest, which would have been fantastic. I'd mentioned more than once that I would love to see *Phantom of the Opera* amongst others. What I absolutely wasn't expecting to find in the envelope, not in a million years, was an online booking slip confirming return flights to Australia.

Six faces watched me, obviously waiting for a reaction,

and I could see that five at least were more than a little apprehensive about what that reaction was going to be. So this was Alice's idea then; as usual she was assuming she knew best.

'What's this, then?' I kept my tone even only by making a supreme effort.

'Well, we thought you'd spent so many years making us all into a proper family that it's given you no time at all to keep in contact with your own,' Alice spoke brightly, and though she seemed sincere I couldn't help feeling there was a slightly malicious edge to her attempt to manipulate me back into a relationship my family and I had given up on years ago. I did try to tell myself that I could have been wrong.

'That's a very nice thought,' I managed, determined not to show how angry I was, and wondered how she'd contrived to persuade them to go along with such a dubious idea and to part with such a lot of money. It was money that the youngest in the family, at least, would barely have been able to afford.

'It's in the Easter holidays so you don't have to worry about your classes,' Mai pointed out. She still looked anxious, and I wondered how hard Alice had worked to convince them all that this was exactly what I would want.

'Lovely,' I managed. Thrusting the envelope into my bag I somehow got through the rest of an evening from which, for me, all the pleasure had gone.

Thankfully, when we arrived home and pulled into the driveway, we could all see lights on in Arthur's house, indicating that his son had arrived, so I went straight round there. Connor, Ella and Mai were right on my heels, probably in case I came face to face with a burglar. It seemed unlikely, though it did cross my mind to wonder how Ron came to have a key.

However, there was no doubting that the man who opened the door was related to Arthur because he was, quite simply, a younger version. I liked him very much on sight.

I put out my hand. 'You must be Ron.'

'G'day. You must be Evie.' He beamed and, looking over my shoulder, added, 'and these must be your kids. G'day.'

He opened the door wide and we all traipsed through, though I assured him we weren't stopping.

'Just making sure you have everything you need and letting you know we're just next door. Have you seen your Dad?'

'Only arrived about an hour ago.' Ron picked up a key from the coffee table and held it up for us to see. 'Would you believe, I still have my original key to this place, and it still fits?'

'And your family, are they with you?' I found myself asking all the questions because the children were unusually silent in the presence of this tall, tanned Australian.

He shook his head. 'It seemed like a good idea at the time, bringing them all over, but it's difficult to get flights right after Christmas and, as my lovely wife so rightly pointed out, life in Australia can't just be dropped at a moment's notice. I work for myself, so I can please myself.'

'Well, your dad is going to be so happy to see you.' I smiled. 'He talks about you and your family all the time and with such pride. He's doing really well and should soon be home.

Now, we're going to make ourselves scarce,' I turned and ushered the others, still oddly silent, before me. 'The bed has been freshly made up and you'll need time to sleep off the jet-lag, but I'm right next door. Once you're up and about, come round, any time.'

Ron stood on the step watching us go, so I kept quiet until we reached my own front door. Then, ushering them inside, I said crossly to the children, 'Well, you were a big help, weren't you? No help at all, in fact. It made me wonder how you would have behaved if he had turned out to be a burglar. Come on then, cat got your tongues?'

'I didn't know what to say,' Mai confessed.

'Neither did I,' Ella agreed, 'especially as Arthur probably wouldn't have had his accident if we hadn't become distracted by the snow and kept him waiting on Christmas night.'

'You seemed to be doing quite all right without us anyway,' Connor pointed out. 'I'd have quite liked to ask him about Australia, but it didn't seem like the right time.'

I shook my head despairingly at the three of them and went to put the kettle on. I did wonder if they were going to ask me about Australia and my proposed trip. I dreaded it, because what on earth was I going to say to them? I had already decided, the minute I opened the envelope and viewed the contents, that I wasn't going anywhere near Australia. After all, what would have been the point? I didn't intend to give the matter another thought.

I was up early the following morning and out in the park with Gizmo as soon as it was light. My intention was to be back at home and cooking my departing lodgers a hearty breakfast before they left for their other lives. No one had been stirring when we left, yet the park was already a bustle with dog walkers, all looking exceedingly cheerful despite the chill in the morning air and the frost on the grass.

I was quickly joined by Poppy's owner, and the friendly Boxer dog and Gizmo were soon taking it in turns to sniff the various trees and going off together to meet and greet other four-legged regulars.

I was able to assure everyone who asked that Arthur's operation had gone really well, that he would soon be home and out in the park again, and they were all pleased to hear that his son had arrived.

Walking home with Gizmo, I was feeling at peace with the world and smiling at his efforts to get me to walk faster. He was straining at the lead but was so light that his weight was barely noticeable.

'You look happy.'

I looked up to see Owen coming towards me and immediately realized that that had been why Gizmo was so keen to get ahead. I watched him bounce around Owen's denim-clad legs and then scrabble to be picked up.

'Well, I am. Happy I'm going to get my house back to myself today,' I joked, then added immediately, 'not really. I'm going to miss the children. I like to feel needed.'

He bent to pick up the tiny dog and tucked him securely under his arm. Gizmo managed to look so smug that I found it really funny.

'They'll always need you,' Owen assured me. 'We all will. Did you have a nice walk?'

I laughed and said, 'Yes, I'm getting into this dog-walking lark.' I indicated the Pomeranian snuggled so contentedly under his arm and teased, 'Suits you, sir. Paris Hilton, eat your heart out.'

'Paris who?'

'Don't you ever read the newspapers, Owen? You're such a philistine. She's the celebrity who is famously credited with making these small dogs fashionable.'

'Explains why I never heard of her, then.' He grinned, then explained, 'I only ever read the sports pages.'

'Philistine,' I taunted again. 'What brings you out at this time of the morning, then?

'Two reasons. The first is that I had a suspicion you would be producing a full English breakfast with all the trimmings and thought you might just have enough to feed one more. The second is that my house was already turning into a war zone at first light. It got so bad that the volume was in danger of making my ears bleed. I had a quick shower and here I am.'

'What on earth is going on with those two?' I asked worriedly. 'I thought they were supposed to be in love.'

'Well, if they are they have a mighty funny way of showing it, that's all I can say. They don't seem to be able to agree on a single thing these last few days.'

'Oh, look, there's Ron.' I was quite glad of the distraction because I really didn't know what to say about Alice and Jake. 'You know,' I went on, 'Arthur's son. He arrived last night while we were at the restaurant.' I waved and he waved back and waited by the gate for us. I noticed he was wearing one of Arthur's coats against the chill of the morning, though it was much too small for him and the one button he'd managed to fasten was straining across his chest and looked set to ping undone at any moment.

'G'day,' he greeted us when we reached him.

'Good morning,' I said, adding, 'I didn't expect to see you about so early. Thought you'd be sleeping off the jet-lag until midday at least. This is Owen, by the way … erm … a good friend of mine.'

The two men shook hands, and Ron said, 'I set the alarm for British time because I've been told that's the sensible thing to do. Apparently, if I go to bed at the normal time tonight and resist the urge to take a nap I think I might have cracked it.'

'Well, now that you're up and about, how do you fancy joining us for a traditional full English breakfast? The perfect start to the day and you'd be very welcome,' I assured him.

'Really?' Ron's blue eyes, so very like Arthur's, brightened and he positively beamed. 'That would be great, Evie. I used to love Mum's cooked breakfasts, but haven't had a real English one like it in years. When shall I come round?'

'Whenever you're ready – now, if you like. You'll meet the kids from last night again; they might even have a bit more to say this time. There'll probably be a couple more, as well.' I was sincerely hoping that Alice and Jake had reconciled their differences as I spoke.

'They're all going back to jobs and unis today,' Owen explained. 'You know, after the Christmas break, so peace will reign again.'

'You won't appreciate an interloper sharing your last

meal, surely, and neither will they.' Ron was suddenly looking doubtful and obviously beginning to have second thoughts.

'Nonsense,' Owen said with a laugh. 'The more the merrier, honestly, and we could do with another guy to even the numbers up. The kids will be so keen to hear about Australia that you might start to wonder if you aren't paying a high price for what will undoubtedly be a great breakfast.'

'If you're sure, I'll be round in two minutes,' Ron said, not even trying to hide his eagerness.

'We're sure,' Owen and I said in unison.

Within a very short time Alice, Jake and Ron had all arrived and joined those already sitting round the table. Soon they were chatting easily. Owen was doing stirling work with the toaster and I was busily adding the fried eggs to the loaded plates when the doorbell rang.

'I'll get it,' yelled Connor from the hallway.

I didn't take much notice, expecting it to be one of the neighbours who had taken to popping round to check regularly on Arthur's progress. I knew I could safely leave Connor to deal with that. I had a heaped plate in each hand and was making my way to the table with them when I looked up to find Stuart standing in the doorway.

I was taken aback, not expecting him to make an appearance; then I clearly remembered saying I would be busy seeing the children off and we could meet up after they'd left.

'Oh, hi,' I managed. 'Wasn't expecting to see you today, was I?'

He didn't reply, just stood there surveying the noisy party sitting round the table chattering and laughing, me with my plates of food, and Owen buttering toast as if his life depended on it.

In the end I put the plates down in front of the intended recipients, and went back for more, saying over my shoulder, 'You're welcome to join us, Stuart. Connor, bring the folding chair from my office.'

'Don't bother,' he said coldly. 'It looks to me as if everyone was welcome *except* me.'

'We're just having breakfast,' I said evenly, bringing more plates to the table and noticing how the conversation around it had dried up. 'Remember, I did tell you that the children are leaving today.'

'And who is the extra guest?'

Ron stood up and put his hand out across the table. 'I'm Ron,' he said. 'Pleased to meet you.'

The hand was ignored and suddenly I was very tempted to empty the next plate I picked up over Stuart's arrogant head.

'Ron is Arthur's son. Remember Arthur from next door, Stuart? Ron arrived from Australia last night.' I gave Stuart the filthiest look I could dredge up as I made the introduction.

'Oh,' he said. Belatedly recollecting his manners he put out his hand at long last and said, 'Pleased to meet you. Arthur is a great guy.'

The chair was brought and Stuart joined the crowd round the table. Soon he was tucking into his hastily assembled breakfast with every appearance of enjoyment. His previous ill-humour seemed to have entirely vanished – along with my appetite. Even the hot, sweet tea Owen had placed in front of me couldn't disguise the very sour taste Stuart's behaviour had left in my own mouth.

Nineteen

In the end it was a very sociable and even enjoyable meal – thanks mostly, I would have to say, to Ron. Every bit as charming as his father, he kept us entertained with tales of life down under. He seemed to have no regrets over his decision to emigrate as a young man – apart from the fact that his own parents had been left behind.

'It was the other way around for you, Mum, wasn't it?' Alice said, bringing up a subject I would have much preferred her to leave alone – as if the airline tickets weren't enough, I thought bitterly. She then went airily on to explain my family history, 'Her parents and sister went to live in Australia and Mum stayed at home because she had just married our biological father.'

Of course, once that much had been said the whole sorry story had to be brought out into the open. How Kevin had upped and left me with the three children, how I was here in England with no support to be had from my own family, or even Kevin's, because they had opted out of our lives when he had, and any friends I had were all busy with their own families.

'It was much the same for me,' Owen clarified for Ron's benefit. 'My parents were elderly and still living in the wilds of Scotland when Susan died suddenly, leaving me with two young children.'

'Oh,' said Ron. 'I thought you were all one family.'

'You'd be pardoned for thinking so,' Stuart muttered, but still loud enough to be heard.

'Yes, you might be,' I snapped, glaring at him, '*if* we hadn't always been so honest – with our children and with anyone else whose concern it was. We got together out of necessity and gave the children a stable upbringing between us. It meant we didn't have to try to get by anymore, depending on expensive and unreliable child minders or the benefit system. The arrangement worked perfectly for us all but I can state categorically that Owen and I are not a couple and we never have been.'

I glanced at Stuart and was surprised by the look of such clear disbelief on his face that I felt as if I'd been punched in the stomach – so hard that it took my breath clean away. I felt such a fool, because I'd truthfully thought that he'd believed me when I said, more than once, that there was not – and never had been – anything of an intimate nature between Owen and me. He'd *said* he believed me, but clearly he had been lying and had had carried on harbouring his doubts all along.

'Well,' said Ron, 'I think you should both be congratulated, because that's the most admirable thing that I ever heard in my life. You've obviously done a grand job between you,' he beamed round the table at the children, 'because you have a bonzer family who are a real credit to you.'

I could have kissed him.

Connor smirked. 'Oh, yes, we are a pretty special bunch, aren't we?' We all burst out laughing then, with Stuart the one notable and sour-faced exception.

'We're proud of them – all of them.' Owen nodded and, turning to me for confirmation, added, 'Aren't we, Evie? Now they're settled, with their career plans moving along nicely, we're also going our separate ways and getting on with our own lives. Just the way we always planned it.'

'That's right,' I agreed with a sharp look in Stuart's direction. 'The only problem we've had has always been trying to convince other people that our relationship has never been what it seemed. Most have accepted us at face value, but there have always been the doubters and I do get fed up to the back teeth with continually trying to explain something that's always made perfect sense to all of us.'

'That's their problem, I would say,' Ron said firmly. 'I wouldn't allow it to become yours. In fact, I reckon you ought to write a book, you know, all about your unusual circumstances and how it's worked out for you. It would make an amazing story.'

'Mum does write,' Mai chirped up, 'but she writes fiction.'

'That should work perfectly for this story then,' Stuart muttered into his cup. It was all I could do not to ask him outright and in front of everybody just what the hell his problem was.

Then I remembered that Ron had just said we shouldn't let other people's problems become ours, so I decided to ignore it altogether. I stood up, and starting to clear the table, announced, 'I'm going to get the dishwasher loaded.'

'And I'll help Connor to load his car and then give the girls a lift to the station when they're ready,' Owen said.

Jake opted to go with him, joining us both first in collecting plates, and depositing them in the kitchen. The room started to empty as everyone began to make a move.

'Thanks for the breakfast,' Stuart said, smiling for what seemed like the first time since he'd come through the door. 'I'll pop back later when everyone has gone.'

I couldn't understand how he could change like that. Slipping so easily from being judgemental and disapproving of a family and lifestyle that had absolutely nothing to do with him, and then back to the charming man I had been so close to falling in love with.

I could scarcely bear look at him, and simply said shortly, 'I'm taking Ron to the hospital to see Arthur later, Stuart, and I know how busy you are. I'll see you tomorrow evening, as we already arranged.'

For a minute he looked mutinous and as if he might argue, but then he left without another word and I went back to clearing the table with a feeling of relief that made me question the exact nature of my feeling for him.

To my surprise it was Alice who remained, offering, 'I'll give you a hand, Mum.'

'I should go.' Ron kind of hovered as if he wasn't quite sure what to do with himself.

'Not unless you have things to do.' I paused with a teetering pile of plates in my hands. 'Sit down and I'll put the kettle on. We like having you here, don't we, Alice?'

'Oh, yes,' she said practically beaming, 'and perhaps when we've all left you can talk to Mum about Australia, because for Christmas we booked flights for her to go and visit her family out there. It was all my idea,' she added proudly.

She said it so smugly that I found myself becoming incensed all over again, but this time my annoyance was directed at Alice instead of Stuart. I couldn't help it. Right in front of Ron, who was our guest and who deserved better than to listen to our petty arguments – except this wasn't petty to me – I demanded, 'Why do you do that, Alice?'

'What?'

'Interfere, is what. It's surely for me alone to decide whether or not I want to make contact with the family who as good as deserted me all those years ago – not you.'

Alice took a step back and looked as if I had hit her. 'But this family means so much to you,' she protested. 'I never dreamed you wouldn't want to see your own. I thought that you only lost contact because you were so busy putting us first and didn't mention it in case it made us feel guilty.

'All those years you spent making us into a proper family. A family just like everybody else's with us five children and our two parents. You did it so well we could barely see the join and I really thought you'd lost your own family in the process. You've worked so hard for us that I thought it would be really nice to do something for you and I really thought I'd got it right for once. I had no idea you wouldn't *want* to see them. I can't ever imagine not wanting to see you.'

She was upset – really upset – and I was horrified.

I reached out and took her hand, relieved when she didn't pull away, and looking at her I wondered how on earth I could have got what had clearly been good intentions so wrong.

'I'm so sorry,' I said. 'Please forgive me, Alice. I think I'm only just beginning to realize that my other family is a subject that I'm far too touchy about, and a subject that I've ignored for far too long.'

'Why don't you both come and sit down and let's talk about this?' Ron suggested. 'I know I'm a complete stranger to you all, but I think I can see where you're coming from and I can talk about families parting from a different point of view.'

I sat, and Alice went to make tea. The dishwasher hummed in the background.

'You're very angry with them for leaving you, aren't you?' Ron asked gently and I nodded.

'You stayed in England because…?'

'I was already engaged to Kevin when they decided to go. They stayed just long enough to see me safely married and then they were gone. My sister was younger so she went with them.'

As we spoke Alice was going about the business of making tea so quietly that it would have been easy to forget she was there. Eventually she came and joined us, carrying the tray.

'Were you *always* this angry with them for leaving?'

While I was thinking of an answer, Ron took the cup that Alice passed to him and, adding several spoonfuls of sugar from the bowl she also offered, he stirred briskly.

He smiled his thanks at her, saying, 'You make tea like my dad always did – good and strong, I've missed that.' Then he turned back to me.

'Well, no, not really,' I admitted eventually. 'In the early days I was happy in my marriage, busy with the children, and we kept in touch – mostly by letter because computers weren't as common then and telephone calls were expensive.'

'And then he – Kevin – left,' Alice prompted. I noted the use of his name and knew it was because she didn't think of Kevin as her father; in fact she probably didn't think of him at all, and hadn't done for years. That was because Owen had willingly undertaken the role of surrogate father for all three of my children and had more than earned the right to the title. 'Just up and left all of us out of the blue.'

I nodded. 'I've never felt so alone and frightened and although my parents could sympathize, they were far too far away to be of any practical or emotional help. By then my sister had married and had children and, to me, my parents seemed totally wrapped up in the grandchildren they had on the doorstep. They appeared to me to have little interest in me or mine, or even how I was managing, and that really hurt.'

'What is it you think they could or should have done?' Ron questioned gently.

'Anything would have been nice,' I felt a tear begin to trickle down my face. Alice took my hand and held it tightly, looking as if she might cry, too. 'But they did nothing. I was so afraid, had no idea how I was going to manage. I needed to know they cared. You've come all this way to be with your Dad when he needs you.'

'But I couldn't have done that in the early days. For one thing I wouldn't have been able to afford the trip; we had a young family and I was still establishing my business. To my regret, I didn't even make it for my mum's funeral, for reasons I won't go into, but that doesn't mean I didn't want

to be here. I'm sure if you speak to your family they would
tell you that they still feel as guilty as I do – but we make
our decisions for better or worse and then we have to live
with them. In other words sacrifices have had to be made for
the better life we moved to Australia to find.'

'I haven't been seeing things from their point of view, I
suppose,' I found myself admitting, 'only from my own.'

'Maybe you needed someone to be angry at, and the
parents who left you behind were an easy target?' Ron
suggested gently. 'I will just say that because they're not
here, it doesn't mean they don't love and miss you. I adore
my dad and miss him every day.'

'But you've at least kept in touch,' I reminded him. 'After
all this time, is there any real point in me trying to rebuild
very ancient bridges?'

'Well, like my dad, your parents are getting older, and
there will come a time when it will be too late to find out the
answer to that question because the chance will be gone. I
can see Dad's accident as my wakeup call and perhaps you
should view your family's Christmas present to you as yours.
A phone call wouldn't hurt, would it?'

It seemed as if we'd been sitting there for ages, but when
everyone came crowding back in to say their goodbyes I realized it had actually been no time at all. It had been just long
enough for the children to pack up the paraphernalia of
university lives in readiness for their various journeys, and
for Ron to point out some cold hard facts and to make me
begin to see things from a perspective apart from my own.

Many hugs and promises from the children to keep in
touch later the house was quiet. Even Ron had returned next

door, but still Alice remained working quietly alongside me to get the house back into some semblance of the neat normality I was used to now that I was living my life alone.

We stripped beds, collected towels and picked up forgotten items with very little being said. I knew she wanted to talk about something – possibly her relationship with Jake or mine with my parents – but I thought it wise to leave it up to her to decide when.

'I thought I would walk Gizmo before I go with Ron to visit Arthur,' I said, as time passed with nothing of any substance being revealed. 'Would you like to come? I usually go to the park.'

'I'd like that.'

We walked side by side, and I glanced at Alice's face more than once in an effort to gauge what was going on behind that very beautiful exterior. Alice had always been the most complicated of the children, prone to moods and to distance herself.

Arthur had been right about her being the eldest, and of an age to be more aware of what was happening when my marriage had failed. I was always conscious that she'd probably taken Kevin's defection very much to heart – and perhaps taken it very personally, too, even blaming herself despite my efforts to persuade her otherwise. Telling her that though Kevin no longer loved me he still loved her had obviously been a non-starter when he had so completely washed his hands of the family he had created. It had taken Owen years of patience to gain her trust completely.

Belatedly, I could see that our recent separation and the packing up of the family home must have rocked her confidence all over again – despite our assurances that nothing else had changed, and the fact she had always known that, one day, it would happen. Perhaps not as grown up as she would have us believe, Alice was obviously more fragile than she chose to appear and the prickly exterior was merely a shield to protect her.

'How do you know when you love someone?' she asked so suddenly and after such a long silence that I actually jumped, being deep in thought myself at that point. 'I mean *really* love them.'

'What kind of love are we talking about?' I managed, bending to let Gizmo off his lead now that we were safely inside the park gates. 'Because there is more than one kind of love and you will love lots of people, in lots of different ways, in your lifetime.'

'Did you love Kevin?'

'Yes, I did,' I answered without hesitation, 'and I still believe he loved me – at least in the beginning.'

'But he left you.'

'Love *can* change, and his obviously did. Perhaps he had difficulty accepting the responsibility as our family grew, because a family brings with it a lot of responsibility, as I'm sure you know only too well in your line of work. Perhaps he found he wasn't ready for that. He isn't the first man to walk away, and he won't be the last. I imagine the only way he could cope with his own actions, once he had made that decision, was to cut all ties. It's the only explanation that I can think of.

'The only way I could cope with what he'd done was to imagine he had died.' I said it bluntly, almost harshly, and realizing probably for the first time how true it was, 'Because although I could accept that he'd left *me* – as I've said, feelings do change and we don't always have control over that – I couldn't accept him turning his back on his three young children. Of course, in the end it truly was his loss and not necessarily ours, because we've all had a pretty good life so far, haven't we?'

Alice nodded enthusiastically, tucked her hand in the crook of my arm, gave it a squeeze and really smiled. I didn't think I could remember a time when it wasn't me instigating touching and hugs when it came to Alice; it felt very good indeed.

'What about Owen, Mum? Do you love him at all?'

'Oh, yes,' I said instantly and without thought. 'What's not to love? He's the loveliest man in the world, but if you're going to ask if I am *in* love with him, the answer is no, Alice, and it always has been.'

'Stuart?'

'Too soon to say – but I am attracted to him.' I almost added: *sometimes*, but realized that would just complicate what should be a simple answer and this was really about Alice, not about me.

'I think,' she said slowly, carefully looking ahead and not at me, 'that I do love Jake, but I'm pretty sure now that I'm not in love with him – or really attracted to him either. There's no fizz of excitement when I see him; there never has been and I feel there should be. I feel that something important is missing. I enjoy his company but I don't crave it. In fact, I think I feel about him the way you've explained that you feel about Owen, but I have no idea how to tell him that when he's obviously expecting so much more.'

I thought about the rows, the icy atmosphere between them lately, and the hurt look in Jake's eyes when Alice snapped at him yet again, and I almost pointed out that he might already have realized.

'Why don't you tell him what you've just told me?' I suggested tentatively in the end, 'and I'm sure I don't need to ask you to please do it kindly. Use Owen and me as an example, if you like. Growing up together has probably confused the issue because the two of you have always been the closest out of the five of you. Perhaps you just felt safe being with him, you know, after all the changes there have been lately.'

'Maybe, I certainly don't ever want to lose Jake as a friend.'

'Be sure to tell him that, then.' I called Gizmo, put him back on the lead, and we headed for home.

Alice was silent for a while, then she stopped right there in the middle of the pavement and gave me a hug. 'Thanks, Mum,' she said, 'for everything. I think I can accept now how much you deserve your own life. I promise to stop harassing you about anyone you want to date or about how you choose to deal with your parents.'

It felt as if I had been through an emotional wringer, what with one thing and the other, and visiting Arthur with Ron brought some much needed light relief into the day. I think his delight in seeing his son was enough to lift the spirits of everyone in his ward, it certainly lifted mine, and I was so impressed that Arthur never, not even for a minute, allowed Ron to feel guilty for his long-ago decision to leave his home country for pastures new. I had known from the moment I'd met Arthur that I could probably learn a lot from him, but I'd never realized quite how much until then.

Ron insisted on buying fish and chips for us both on the way home from the hospital, and we ended up sharing the traditional meal at my dining room table, chatting easily and making plans for Arthur's imminent discharge from hospital. After he'd left I sat in a silence that seemed foreign after the bustle of Christmas as I contemplated my next move. It had grown late, but, calculating that it was already well into the next day in Australia, I reached first for the pretty address book that held all the telephone numbers of family and friends, then I reached for the phone.

As the telephone began to ring in another country the receiver almost slipped from a hand that had quickly become slick with perspiration. The longer it rang the more relieved I felt as the realization dawned that there was nobody at home to take my call and I could leave this until another time.

I had even begun to take the instrument from my ear to disconnect the call, when a voice, disconcertingly familiar, said, 'Hello.'

'Dad,' I said, 'it's me. It's—'

'Evie,' he said, and we both burst into tears.

Twenty

In the end the conversation I had dreaded, avoided and insisted I had no interest in for so long was not at all how I had imagined would be. There were no recriminations on either side, just a willingness to forgive and forget whatever grudges we had been harbouring and to become a family again, despite the distance. It was as if the weight I'd refused to acknowledge I'd been carrying for so long had been lifted from my shoulders as the warm words of my parents made it easy to imagine I was enveloped in the loving arms I suddenly remembered so well.

Alice was the first one I spoke to on the following morning, eager to share the news that I'd telephoned Australia and that all was well with me and my parents, and that they were keen to hear from their grandchildren in England, too. I put aside the guilty knowledge that my behaviour had been instrumental in curtailing that contact as well, because the children had obviously followed my lead and shown no interest in the only grandparents they had.

It was time to look forward and not back, as I told Alice,

and I was so pleased that I had rung her to share my news because, besides showing her pleasure for me, she was able to tell me that she'd had a long and very honest talk with Jake the previous evening. He had accepted with equanimity everything that she had said, and seemed relieved, she said, to return their relationship to what it always had been. Perhaps they had both realized they weren't couple material. I knew only too well that it would be all too easy to mistake friendship for love and I was glad all over again that Owen and I had been careful not to make that error of judgement.

I was ready when Stuart called for me that evening. He was all smiles and quite back to his usual very charming self. The good looks that had first attracted me to him were accentuated by the black shirt and jeans he wore with a soft leather jacket of the same colour.

'Evie,' He held me at arm's length, taking in my own black-clad figure in a silk shirt and slim fitting jeans worn with a honey-coloured suede jacket and matching boots. 'You look good enough to eat,' he said approvingly, then he drew me close and kissed me until I was breathless and it was far too easy for me to forget his ill-humour of the previous day.

He held the car door open and helped me into the vehicle as if I was something very precious to him, then chatted easily as he drove, telling me about his day and the place he had chosen to take me for a meal and hoping that I was going to like it.

There was nothing *not* to like in the long, low white-washed building with its charming thatched roof, beamed ceilings and log fires. It had probably started life as a simple country pub and morphed over time into a very popular restaurant, judging by the fact that the only empty table in the place was the one we were shown to.

'This was how I intended us to be,' he confessed as we waited for the first course to arrive, 'when I first asked you out.'

'Us?' I questioned with a smile. 'Isn't it still a bit soon for there to be an "us"?'

'Not for me.' He reached across the table and took my hand in his, and I felt my stomach flip at the warm look in his eyes.

'We haven't actually seen that much of each other so far,' I reminded him gently, when the waiter had taken his time placing the seafood starters in front of us and had then left.

'Well, that wasn't for want of trying on my part,' he reminded me, 'especially once we actually reached Christmas and I could have put work behind me for a while.'

'I know.' I shrugged easily. 'But it's not a great time of the year to be thinking about romance when you have a family – especially this year, with all the changes that the house moves brought. I think it must have made everyone feel a bit insecure.' I shook out my napkin, turned my attention to the starter and tucked in with enjoyment.

'Especially me.'

I looked up and straight at him, smiled carefully and took a sip of my wine, before I said, 'Yes, I noticed you were a bit touchy. What on earth was that all about?'

'Just that you seemed to have time for just about everyone in your life apart from me, and I was starting to take it personally.'

'Well, Arthur's accident wasn't planned and neither was your reaction to finding Owen in my house when you called for me the following morning but, thanks to Alice, we did see each other on Boxing Day evening.

'I don't recall inviting you to join us for breakfast yesterday, but I'm sorry if you felt unwelcome. I did say the children would be going back to university and work and I wanted to spend time with them before they left.' I said this calmly and then carried on eating, refusing to let what he was saying get to me. 'You can have me all to yourself now, if that's what you want.'

The first course dishes were removed and the main course was brought almost immediately. I picked up my knife and fork, determined to enjoy the lamb shank and creamy mashed potato.

'Until the next holiday,' Stuart sounded gloomy.

'But, Stuart, you always knew I had five children. It was hardly kept a secret from you.'

'That's it, though, isn't it?' he said triumphantly. 'You don't have five children – you're the mother of *three*.'

I still kept my attention on my meal, though the enjoyment was definitely beginning to pall, and my voice was steady as I replied, keeping my tone firm, 'To all intents and purposes, Stuart, I am the mother of *five*, and that will never change.'

'OK,' he agreed, obviously knowing when he was beaten and making an obvious effort to accept it, 'but it's not just the children, is it? There's Arthur, and now his son, and Owen is forever on the scene. I practically trip over the guy every time I come to your house. I mean, I thought that was all over between you two.'

'*That?*' Even I could hear the hard note that had crept into my tone.

'You know.'

'No,' I said, 'I'm afraid I don't know.' I could feel myself becoming very, very annoyed.

He was silent then, perhaps realizing for the first time that he had gone too far. We ate without speaking for a while, and normally that would be fine, but all enjoyment in the food, delicious as it had been, had completely gone for me and there was a tension in the air that could have been cut with a knife.

In the end Stuart gave up first. He pushed his plate away and said, 'I know what you've said, Evie, but you must admit, it is pretty hard to swallow the fact that you and Owen lived together for fifteen years – *fifteen*, Evie – and I'm expected to believe that nothing of a remotely intimate nature ever happened between you.'

'Do you know,' I said, placing my knife and fork neatly side by side on the plate and then throwing down my napkin beside it, 'I actually expect you to believe whatever it is you damn well please, Stuart. It's actually not my job to convince you. I don't even care any more what you believe, because you obviously choose not to believe *me*. Why on earth would I lie about such a thing? Why? Tell me that.'

Challenged like that Stuart didn't seem to know what to say.

'What exactly are you expecting from me – a *confession*? Why would I feel the need to confess to you about something that – even if it was true – is quite clearly in my past? Why would I bother to hide it if Owen and I did have a sexual relationship all these years because, Stuart, that would be absolutely none of your business.'

'So you did,' he began, looking ridiculously pleased to have scored some sort of point.

'Do you know what?' I said, finally exasperated beyond bearing, 'Think what you like, because I really couldn't care less. Waiter?' I raised my hand and my voice, 'Can we have the bill, please?'

'Oh, no, Evie, don't be like that.' It seemed to dawn on Stuart, rather belatedly, that he might just have completely overstepped the mark. 'Look, I'm sorry, really sorry. Please sit down. Come on, you must admit it is a hard story to swallow.'

I sat down, though it was the last thing I felt like doing. I was angry, hurt, very, very disappointed and extremely sad that something so promising was falling apart right in front of my eyes, and all for no good reason as far as I could see.

'As I've already said, I couldn't live with you for fifteen *days* without trying it on,' Stuart said in an extremely feeble effort to turn the whole sordid thing into a joke that he must know I was never going to find the least bit funny.

'Well,' I said emphatically, 'as I'm sure I've said before, I think that says far more about you than it does about Owen, and I'll ask you again, why on earth would I feel the need to lie about my and Owen's relationship to you or anybody else? It would have been far easier over the years to just let everyone think what they liked – just as most of them did. Instead we tried to be totally honest and risked being pooh-poohed because it seemed important to us, and even more to our children, that we tell the truth no matter what.'

'OK, OK, I'm prepared to accept that you're telling the truth because, after all, as you've said, why would you lie?' Even as Stuart spoke I could tell that he was the one who was lying, but I could no longer be bothered to challenge him, especially when he continued: 'It's not just about Owen, though, is it? Although I have to say he never seems to be off your doorstep these days and I find that disconcerting enough. I'd have thought you had enough to do with the five children but, as I said before, now there's Arthur and even his son whom you've taken under your wing.'

I decided not to throw the very recent contact with my family in Australia into an already complicated equation, or even the thawing of relationships with the neighbours in the close, but just said mildly, 'Don't you have any friends in your life, Stuart?'

He laughed shortly, 'Well, I don't *collect* them like you do, that's for sure. What I would like to know is when are you going to find time for your writing and time for me?'

'Things will settle down, especially now the children are more or less off my – our – hands. Real life often means squeezing things in and some things do have to take priority over others at times. That's life – especially family life, I'm afraid.'

'It's not *my* life,' Stuart said bluntly, and I realized then that it was over between us. All I could feel was an over-whelming and immense sense of relief.

The journey home wasn't comfortable and I had the feeling that Stuart was surprised – even shocked – when I didn't immediately offer promises to give more time to our relationship, or indicate that I would make a bigger effort to become what he wanted. The truth was that I came with a family and friends, with responsibilities, that I couldn't – and wouldn't – just ignore, and I wasn't going to apologise for that.

I gathered Gizmo into my arms as soon as I had closed the front door behind me, and told him, as I fended off a frenzy of licking, 'I'm surprised he didn't complain about the amount of time I spend with you, Gizzie. You know what, little one? Somehow I don't think I will miss him very much, after all, but I *am* going to miss you.'

It wasn't horrendously late, since the evening with Stuart had been abruptly cut short, so I clipped on the little dog's lead and made my way to the park. It was well lit and well-populated with dog-walkers, and I felt quite safe. I knew I was going to miss Gizmo's company a lot, not to mention the regular walks, though it was good news that Arthur was in fine fettle and returning home tomorrow as good as new.

'Ah,' a familiar voice behind me said, making me jump a little, 'I thought I would find you here as soon as I realized the dog was missing.'

'Checking up on me, Owen?' I said lightly, but for once it didn't bother me, probably because I'd finally accepted that he just cared about me, the same way I would always care about him.

'Not at all, I'd been out for a pint with Ron and saw that your lights were on when I dropped him off. Back early, aren't you?'

'Mmm,' I agreed, shortly and without comment, but he obviously picked up on something: maybe the negative vibe.

'It's not us, is it – me and the children causing a problem?

Especially me, actually, now I think about it, because I can understand that not many guys will want an ex hanging around.'

'But strictly speaking you're not an ex, are you, given the fact we've never been in a relationship,' I pointed out.

'Try explaining *that*,' he said with a hint of bitterness.

'Oh, I *have*, believe me, I have.'

'You, too, Evie? I'm so sorry.'

'Do you know what?' I stopped suddenly and turned to him in the middle of the path. Gizmo had been trotting ahead but now he gave up on sniffing a tree and came running back to see what was going on. 'You have absolutely nothing to apologize for and neither do I. What we've had all these years has been great and we've had the happiest of times – despite the perhaps unusual circumstances.

'After all,' I went on, 'our relationship was never complicated to us or to the children – and they should know how things were between us if anyone should. I'm finally done with explaining and I will never again feel myself under an obligation even to begin to apologize for having got family life so absolutely right.'

Owen stared at me, then we both burst out laughing, hugged and, arm in arm, with Gizmo securely back on his lead, we made our way home.

New Year's Eve found me wending my way the few steps next door to Ruth and Giles's bungalow. Like Arthur's on the other side of mine, these homes had originally been built on very similar lines. Mine had been extended slightly upwards into the roof space and an addition had been added to the back that housed the sitting room end of my open plan living space, but this one appeared to have been almost tripled in size with various extensions, both up and out, and with a smart conservatory added into the bargain. I couldn't wait to see how it all looked from the inside and rang the doorbell eagerly.

'Evie, how lovely to see you! Do come inside.'

It was Ruth who threw the door open wide and I was immediately glad that I had made a bit of extra effort over my appearance. Her fair hair was drawn severely back from a face that was meticulously made up. Her floor-length black off-one-shoulder dress, I was ready to swear, came from none of the well-known high street chains, unlike my own which had been purchased in the Monsoon pre-January sale and had been an absolute snip.

However, I felt I could hold my own and shimmied inside on my gold killer heels, pleased with my scarlet ensemble, set off by matching dangly earrings that were shown to advantage by my upswept hairdo. For once, I felt I had got it right and was pleased I hadn't opted for something more casual.

Several neighbours were already inside and I was delighted when Arthur and Ron arrived close behind me. I watched as they were both soon surrounded by well-wishers, all extremely keen to offer help and support should Arthur need it in the future. Gizmo had now been returned to his rightful owner and though I was more than happy that this should be so, I missed that little dog more than I could ever have imagined. However, I was very careful not to say so and just made a promise to myself that

I would seriously consider a small pet of my own in the New Year.

'And what about that lovely man of yours? Is he coming?' It was the elderly lady whose name I could never remember who lived the other side of Arthur. 'Owen, isn't it?'

I automatically opened my mouth to correct her, then, remembering my recent conversation with Owen, I thought better of it.

'It is Owen, yes, and I'm sure he will be here shortly.'

In fact, as the time went on and there was still no sign of Owen, I started to wonder if he was all right. He had promised not to be late and it wasn't like Owen to miss a party. He had seemed keen enough yesterday when I'd reminded him about the invitation to this one.

A lively discussion was taking place in the group I had become attached to, about the shortcomings of the refuse collection service of all things, and as my mind drifted I found myself trying to recall what Owen's plans had been for the day. It was when I remembered he'd said he was going to be working on his own that I really started to worry.

I told myself not to be so fanciful, that he had probably just changed his mind and was even now sharing a drink with the lady he had been seeing. Try as I might to dismiss it, though, the thought that something had happened to him kept coming back to torment me. What if a wall had toppled onto him? What if he'd drilled into an electric cable? He could have fired his nail gun, hit an artery and even now be lying somewhere bleeding to death.

I began to seriously worry and imagine a whole host of worst-case scenarios and cursed the fact I hadn't brought my mobile phone. A minuscule evening bag, while very pretty, was worse than useless, being filled to capacity with only my key and a lipstick inside. As more time passed, reminding myself that I was being ridiculous didn't seem to be helping.

'I thought Owen said he was coming tonight.' Ron came over to me, looking disappointed. He checked his watch. 'He'll miss seeing the New Year in if he doesn't hurry.'

I almost kissed the big Australian, because he had just given me the excuse I needed to check up on Owen.

I smiled, as if I wasn't a bit concerned, but said, 'I'll go and give him a ring for you, Ron. Just to see where he is. I won't be a minute.'

Something was wrong, I just knew it was. I felt sick and wondered what on earth the children would do if something happened to Owen – and what I would do.

I flew down the garden path as fast as my heels and flowing skirt would allow me, through the gate – and smack into Owen's arms.

'Hello,' he held me steady and laughed down at me, 'where are you off to in such a hurry?'

'Oh,' I said, 'you! Where have you *been*, Owen? You should have been here hours ago. Everyone's been asking after you,' I was grossly exaggerating in my anger and I didn't even care. 'Oh,' I huffed childishly, 'I'm surprised you bothered to come at all, since you obviously preferred someone else's company. You should have stayed to see the New Year in with *her*.' Then I thoroughly disgraced myself by bursting into tears and confessed, 'I was getting so worried.'

'Evie, I wasn't with anyone else.' He looked down at me, his blue gaze gentle and very warm. 'I just lost track of time and then carried on to get the job done. You must know it was never going to work for me with any "someone else". I tried a couple of dates with someone, but it was really over even before it had begun.'

'It was?' I peeped back up at him. 'Why?'

'Because she wasn't you,' he said simply. It was only then that I realized why it hadn't worked for Stuart and me, either.

'Oh,' I said.

We stared at one another as if we hadn't really seen each other before. Perhaps we hadn't, because all we had craved in those early difficult days together was stability and a safe environment for our wounded selves and for the children who depended on us to hold everything together.

We had spent the last fifteen years insisting our relationship wasn't what it seemed; now, in less than fifteen minutes, we had realized at last that it was fast becoming exactly what it seemed. The fireworks exploding and the bells ringing when we kissed were an unexpected bonus

'Happy New Year,' someone called and we smiled at each other.

'I don't think there's any doubt about that,' I said.